Ros Baxter fiction.

Her titles include *Fish Out of Water* and *White Christmas*, and she co-authored *Sister Pact* with her sister Ali. She has also been a contributing author to the e-anthology URL Love. Sequels to *Sister Pact* and *Fish Out of Water* will be published in 2014, as well as a new romantic comedy: *Lingerie for Felons*.

Ros lives in Brisbane, Australia, with her husband Blair, four small but very opinionated children, a neurotic dog and nine billion germs.

Second Chances

ROS BAXTER

PAN

Pan Macmillan Australia

First published 2014 in Pan by Pan Macmillan Australia Pty Ltd
1 Market Street, Sydney, New South Wales, Australia, 2000

Cataloguing-in-Publication entry is available
from the National Library of Australia
http://catalogue.nla.gov.au

ISBN: 9781742613727

Based on the television series by Bradley P. Bell
Story Editor, Rhonda Friedman

Printed in Australia by McPherson's Printing Group

Papers used by Pan Macmillan Australia Pty Ltd are natural,
recyclable products made from wood grown in sustainable forests.
The manufacturing processes conform to the environmental
regulations of the country of origin.

To Jacqueline MacInnes Wood. Best. Steffy. Ever.

Chapter One

Steffy looked at her glistening body in the mirrored wall as she stepped out of the bath. Suds clung to her skin and the heady smell of the bath salts she'd brought back from Paris perfumed the air. Her breasts were still round and full, but she was thinner than she'd been in a long time, and her hand went automatically to her belly, cradling it protectively. She snatched it away, reaching for a thick white towel and rubbing at her skin viciously.

No moping.

She donned a peach-colored negligee and stepped out to her desk, sitting down to try, once again, to transfer the pictures in her mind onto paper. She ran her fingers over the desk's warm, dark surface as she looked out the sheer glass wall over the skyline, imagining other fingers tracing the same path over the last three centuries. The wood felt solid and real, an antidote to the madness and shifting loyalties of LA. Her father had seen her eyes light up when she spotted the beautiful piece back in Paris. And so it had followed her home.

She tapped a pencil on the sketchpad. The excitement of the spring fashion shows in Paris had awakened something in her—a stirring to bring the color and light of the Left Bank to LA. She had felt once again the rush of wanting to create a new line for Forrester Creations—Europe on the West Coast. But tonight there was only one thing on her mind.

She tried to focus on the sketch already on the pad. The outfit was cute, its upturned collar and simple bodice flowing down to a pencil skirt with a flouncy fishtail. But it wasn't the piece that caught her eye, it was the face of the model. She was gaunt, dark eyes staring into the distance as though they were looking for a way to escape. Steffy looked back to the window and caught her own reflection staring back at her from the glass. She looked like the model. Gaunt, haunted—looking for a way out.

She had sketched herself.

Steffy stood up, tearing the top page from the sketchpad and crumpling it before tossing it into the overflowing trash basket. As she did, a loud hammering interrupted her thoughts. Strange for someone to come calling at this hour.

She moved to the door, and pressed the intercom. "Who is it?"

"Me. I've come to pick up some things. Can I come in?" Liam's voice was low and dark, his light drawl slightly slurred. She wondered if he'd been drinking.

"I—" Steffy rubbed her arms where they were still cool from the light breeze that had been coming in from the balcony. She looked down at her lacy negligee and considered stopping by her room for a wrap before letting him in. Then she shook the thought away and opened the door. "Come in," she said, ushering him through with one arm. "Are you okay?"

Liam ran his long fingers through his hair. He was wearing it shorter and it made him look younger, but the fine lines around his eyes suggested weariness. She drew in a deep breath, closing her eyes and thinking about the last time she and Liam had spoken. Two weeks ago, only a few days after Steffy had stepped off the plane.

Tonight the effect he had on her was frustrating and predictable. Her breath hitched and her heart rate spiked as she watched him standing uncertainly in the foyer. Her fingers itched to reach out and smooth his ruffled hair, bring him in toward her and hold him close, whispering soothing things. But he had no right to her sympathy. He had not been there for her.

She would not be there for him.

She cursed herself for the effect he had on her. In many ways, this man was like the other half of her, so close and familiar. But they were as lethal to each other as they had been essential to each other's survival.

She watched his eyes roam over her face and body, taking in the negligee, and she raised her chin, determined now that she would definitely not fetch a robe. This was her home, for now at least, and if she had to endure the physical impact of this man on her, then he would have to put up with her physical impact on him too.

She stood, waiting for him to speak first, but he continued to stare at her.

"You look tired," he said finally, his voice catching slightly. "And beautiful."

The words hit her like a blow to the stomach. Her hands automatically hugged her waist, like they were trying to protect her from the spell Liam could always spin to bring her back to him.

"Yeah, well," she said lightly, "you actually look kind of drunk."

He laughed, and her tummy clenched and her skin heated up at the dizzying sexiness of it. The rich, throaty sound played havoc with her brain and her ability to breathe.

"Not drunk enough," he said, walking to the refrigerator and retrieving a bottle of wine.

She raised an eyebrow at him, and he stared her down as he lounged against the kitchen bench.

He extracted a corkscrew from a drawer before pulling the cork with a gentle pop. "Join me?"

His eyes were dark and inviting and Steffy's mind warned her that this was dangerous ground. They had too much to resolve before they could drink wine and make eyes at each other.

"No, thanks," she said, as politely firm as she could be.

"Aw, come on, Steffy," he said. "I promise I don't bite." The sentence drew her eyes to his mouth, and she remembered how it felt on her skin, playing across her breasts. He did bite, sometimes, she remembered—but only when she really wanted him to.

He shrugged, looking boyish and dangerous all at once. "I'll get my things soon. I … I just want to talk. We have some things to talk about, don't you think?"

She nodded. "Yes. And don't you think we might be better off talking about them when you're sober, and I'm fully dressed?"

"No, I don't," Liam said, and his eyes flashed at her, sweeping over her nightgown and lingering on her cleavage, showing just how clearly he approved of what he saw there.

Steffy considered her options. She could ask him to leave, and he probably would. But she wanted to know what he was thinking. And perhaps, like this, she would learn more from him than she ever would when he was completely sober. He was usually so careful and in control.

Or she could get dressed, and then continue the conversation. But for some reason, she liked the steamy looks he was giving her nightgown. She'd been driven mad these last two weeks, wondering where he was, who he was with, whether he was missing her. And, most of all, if it was Hope who was consoling him.

To have him here felt good. It felt right. Even if he was her husband in name only.

Even if they had ended it before she went to Paris two months ago.

And then ended it again two weeks ago.

But while he was here, watching her hungrily, he wasn't somewhere planning a new future with Hope.

She sat, then nodded at him. "Okay," she said.

Liam pulled two large glasses down from the rack and Steffy closed her eyes to enjoy the sound of the wine filling them.

When she looked at Liam again, he was watching her. "Why did you go to Paris?"

His gaze was holding Steffy's so intently she couldn't pull loose. He looked so boyish, and confused, she couldn't decide if she wanted to kiss him or throw him out.

"Oh, Liam," Steffy sighed. "You know as well as I do how bad things were between us when I left for Paris."

"But I thought we worked all that out." It was almost a whine. "You came home. You came back to me."

"I didn't know what else to do," Steffy said. And it was the truth. Liam had called her after she had fled to Paris, begging her to come home, to give them another chance.

"I've tried," Liam said. "I did just like you asked. I didn't tell anyone you were home, I got this place for us so we could take our time ..."

"I tried too," Steffy said. "When I saw you there, waiting at the airport for me with that huge bunch of roses." Steffy could not help but smile at the memory. Liam, wearing the smile he saved only for her. She had really believed they could make it work too. Those mischievous brown eyes and that wicked grin had made her knees weak as she'd stumbled into the warmth of his embrace, feeling strong arms wrap protectively around her. He'd put his mouth against her hair, breathed her in, and whispered in her ear, "You're home now, and everything's going to be okay, Steffy."

But it was far from okay. They'd known that within days of her return.

Her hand moved again to her belly. "You really don't get it, do you?" Her breath burned, hot and sour, in her throat. "I lost my baby," she whispered, working hard to stay in control of her voice and her self-control. "Our baby."

He nodded, finally tearing his eyes from hers and staring at the marble floor.

The urge to wound him rose full and powerful in her heart. "But I lost more than that. I lost everything. I lost *you*." Her skin buzzed with pain at the memory of it. "You could barely speak to me, barely look at me. And I lost something else, too." She stared at him, willing him to bring his eyes to hers. "Don't you remember?"

He continued to stare at the floor. Curse him.

"I lost the chance of ever being a mother. Have you any idea how that feels?"

He finally looked up at her, but he shook his head again. Of course he didn't know how that felt. He couldn't.

"It's the kind of grief that tears at you. The kind of grief that wakes you up at night." She tossed her head. "I thought I knew all about grief. After losing Phoebe—" As she mentioned her sister's name, Steffy's voice became ragged and stiff in her throat. She ploughed on. "After Phoebe, and after the baby, I thought I knew all about grief. But when they told me—" Hot, fat tears blurred her vision.

Liam reached for her hand but she shook it away, picking up her wine and taking a long pull of it. "When they told me I would never, ever have a baby, I knew a whole other kind of grief. Sometimes it's so bad it makes me feel like I'm going crazy. I never even thought I wanted a baby.

But—" The words formed in her brain before they spilled from her mouth, and she almost considered stopping herself. After all, she could have been talking about the two of them. "But sometimes you don't know what you've got till it's gone."

Liam stared hard at her. "I know what you mean," he said. "I know exactly what you mean." He reached a hand up to rub Steffy's arm, then stood and moved toward her, trying to pull her into his arms.

He was close, tantalizingly close. And it would be so easy to surrender to him, to let him pull her into his arms, as he had a thousand times before, and make it all right. He smelled exactly right; he looked exactly right. He was her Liam. Hers.

She started to sway toward him, and stopped herself. This was important. It was important that he understand.

He hadn't understood after the miscarriage.

He hadn't understood three weeks ago, when she had returned from Paris and he had wanted to start over as though everything could be the same.

And he hadn't understood a few days later, when she'd thrown him out.

She needed him to hear this. "I thought you would be different when I got back from Paris. I thought the blame would have gone out of your eyes. But when I looked at you, I still saw it there."

Liam stepped back a little from Steffy, but he didn't meet her eyes.

"You can't deny it, Liam, I know it's true." As Steffy said the words, she felt the truth of them settle into her skin.

"It's not." Liam stalked around the kitchen bench, refilling his glass with shaking fingers before banging the wine bottle down. "Steffy, I—"

"Say it then." Steffy stood and moved closer to him, leaning on her side of the bench. The cold marble between them felt just right, just like the place they had come to in their relationship, separated by something so big and cold and frightening they didn't know how to overcome it. "Say you don't blame me for our baby dying."

Liam shrugged, and tipped the glass to his mouth, taking long swallows. "Things happen, Steffy," he said. "It isn't always fair. It isn't always …" He trailed off, and Steffy saw the avoidance in his eyes.

Time stretched as she stared him down.

"You can't say it," she said. "Because it isn't true. You do blame me. You blame me for getting on the motorbike that day. And you'll never forgive me for it. And you'll never forget it. Just like I'll never forget how it felt, when I went to find you, to tell you about our baby—and saw you with Hope. *Kissing* Hope."

As she said the words, the scene replayed in her head as it had a million times, over and over in slow motion. The two of them, wrapped in each other. Liam, her Liam, her husband. And that woman who would never, ever, let him go. Even in that moment, the moment that should have belonged to her and Liam, Hope was there, ruining her joy, stealing her happiness.

Right now, she wanted to wound him as he had wounded her that day. "There are some things we can't rewind, Liam, no matter how badly we might want to."

Liam ran his hands through his hair. "I don't blame you," he said, still avoiding her eyes. "But maybe," he started, then stopped and cleared his throat, like he was trying to get it right. "Maybe everything happens for a reason. Maybe this was meant to be. You never wanted to be a mother. You never wanted a baby."

Oh no. No, no, no.

How dare he? How dare he try to make this horrible thing somehow fated? This thing that had ripped out her heart? Was he really trying to say that her baby had died because she was not good enough, didn't want it enough?

"I wanted this baby," Steffy snarled, feeling something big and ugly well inside her chest. "I wanted *our* baby. I would never have deliberately hurt that baby."

"Hey." Liam held up his hands. His brown eyes were soft and warm. "I never thought you deliberately did anything."

"What then?" Steffy could hear her voice building in intensity, becoming more shrill. "You think I was careless? Reckless?"

A change came over Liam's face, and she could see he'd reached tipping point. Suddenly his efforts to placate and understand slipped away. She saw only cold fury in his eyes.

"You just aren't used to thinking about other people, Steffy," he said finally. "You've never had to. It's not in your nature."

Steffy's hand snaked out before she could stop it. She could almost feel the satisfying slap before it connected. She relished it, waiting for the hot connect of skin on skin just like—in another time—she might have waited to feel Liam's lips on hers.

But it never did. Liam's hand shot out and grasped hers, his grip like a manacle on her wrist.

He shook his head at her again. "Okay, you want to hear it, Steffy? You want the truth? Here it is. You should never have gotten on that motorbike. Not knowing you were pregnant. That was my child too, Steffy. And I'm hurting too. You thought you never wanted to be a mother? Well, I'd never thought about it either, till you told me it was gone. And then it was all I could think about. You, with our child. It seemed perfect. Too good to be true."

He grinned ruefully. "And I guess that was exactly what it was." He dropped her hand like it was rattlesnake. "*You're* sad, Steffy? *You're* angry? *You* feel cheated?" He banged his fist on the countertop with each sentence. "Well, guess what? You're not the only one hurting here, Steffy. It's time you grew up, and started to think about how your behavior affects other people."

She had known the truth of it, seen it in his eyes. But he could not possibly know how much it hurt to hear him say it aloud, to feel each barb land in her heart. Surely if he knew what he was doing to her, he would not be doing it like this.

So deliberately, so precisely.

She wanted to scream at him that things were different now. That the girl who had ridden off on that motorbike was gone forever.

That some losses changed you, right in the moment they happened. Changed you in a way you could never undo. She wasn't that same, selfish girl any more.

But why should Liam believe her? And did she even want him to?

Because she had spent so long wanting this man to love her that she could hardly remember anything else in her life.

She closed her eyes, trying to block out a red swirl of pain.

What hurt most of all was that she could see in his face that he didn't know. He had no idea what tomorrow was. And why tonight was hard enough anyway, without having to have this conversation right now. He had known her for so long, and he didn't even know this about her.

She pointed to the door. "Go," she said.

Liam picked up his glass and drank the wine slowly, holding Steffy's gaze as he did. His eyes were unreadable, even to Steffy, who had always been able to see exactly what Liam was thinking and feeling by looking at them. "I'll just get my things." He moved over to her bedroom, their bedroom, and Steffy turned back to her desk and the balcony.

She flicked a tiny button on a small remote control and filled the room with music, the slow, haunting strains of the London Philharmonic. She had seen the Philharmonic in concert several times when she'd been at boarding school in England. Its music reminded her of something else she had lost. And tonight was all about memories.

When Liam strode out of the bedroom, he was carrying a large leather satchel. He stopped by the door.

"Steffy."

She turned from where she'd been facing the balcony, looking out over the skyline again, watching the gaunt face she barely recognized in the reflection of the glass.

Liam was very serious, and still. "I didn't mean for this to happen this way," he said. "I didn't come here to upset you."

She waved a hand at him, trying to seem casual, unaffected. "It doesn't matter. Like I said,

I knew anyway. I shouldn't have asked if I didn't want to hear."

Liam covered the space between them in three long strides. He grasped her upper arms in his hands, shaking her gently. "But it isn't like that, Steffy. I don't—"

Steffy was barely holding it together, and the closeness of this body, the smell of him, like the sea and spice and their shared history, was more than she could bear. Her hands itched to touch him. She knew him so well, adored every inch of him. She would crumple, she would not get through this unless he left now.

"Please go," she said. "I think you've said enough."

Liam dropped his hands and leaned forward to press a light kiss on her cheek. As his lips connected with her skin, she felt the familiar sizzle and ache he was always able to ignite in her.

But no more. She was a different person now. And she needed to be allowed to grow and change. To be defined by something other than her wild, consuming love for Liam Spencer.

"Goodbye, Liam," she said. The words made her throat scratchy and dry. So many goodbyes between them, but perhaps this time, for good. "I need to tell you, I've decided to go back. To Paris, and my father. For a year, maybe more. I need some more time. Before I can face it all here. I …" She paused, wanting him to understand how things were for her. "I'm just not ready. I should never have come home."

Liam's face darkened, his brows shutting down and his eyes narrowing. "Were you even going to tell me?"

She nodded. She couldn't speak. Not with her throat closing over, and her heart burning in her chest.

"Why did you come back at all?" His face was hard, and it took all Steffy's strength not to run to him, to try to explain. He should *know*. He should know this about her.

"For Phoebe," she whispered.

"Phoebe?" His voice was soft and the dark mask finally lifted a little. "Your sister ...? But why?"

As he asked the question, Steffy saw the answer dawn on him.

"Oh, Steffy," he said, stepping towards her. He held out his arms to her and she wanted to run into them like a child, bury her face in his chest and sob. But then they would be right back where they had started. Where they always ended up.

"Goodbye, Liam," she said.

He stood still for a moment, indecision in every line of his face and body. Then he turned and made for the door.

She walked to the trifolds leading out onto the balcony and slid them open, enjoying the feel of the early summer night air on her skin.

As she stepped out into the LA night, her heart rate began to settle. The lights and sights of this city always had the power to calm her. She touched the warm skin of her belly through the negligee, thinking about the life that had been growing inside her.

She had never considered herself the maternal type. The sight of women with sticky, screaming babies made her feel lucky that she only had herself to look out for, that she wasn't burdened by caring for something small and helpless.

But all that had changed the moment she had discovered she was carrying a child. Suddenly, it hadn't been an abstract idea. It hadn't been someone else's sticky, irritating burden. It had been her child. Hers and Liam's growing inside her.

She stroked her belly, remembering the brief time she had known about the baby, before the miscarriage. The delicious feeling of belonging to another person, belonging to her baby. And to Liam. The baby made her want things she had never wanted before, a home, a family.

But now Liam had gone and she wondered if this time it was over for good.

A sudden breeze ruffled her hair. It was longer now than when she had left LA and she was wearing it loose and lightly curled, as was the fashion right now in Paris. She shivered as the sudden cool rush brought gooseflesh to her arms, then retreated into the warmth of the apartment.

She spotted the small red folder sitting on the desk. She picked it up and hugged it to her chest. Her tickets and itinerary. She knew now her instincts were right. She was going back to Paris, for longer this time. The things she had said to Liam were right. It had been a mistake to come home so quickly, on Liam's urging. She just wasn't ready. She was leaving in a few days, to be with her father, walk in the sunshine. Heal. Forget. Hopefully forget.

But could she ever forget Liam?

*

It was the same as always.

Her head was full of cotton and thick, black fear, smoky and ugly.

Steffy was trying to warn her sister. *Get out of the car.*

She was back there, where she had been six years ago, when she'd had the feeling. And this time, instead of ignoring that prickly itch that told her when her twin was in danger, she had listened to it. In this dream, she had called Phoebe, demanded she get out of the car.

But Phoebe could not hear her—*would not* hear her. She was full of fury and lashing out at Rick. Steffy could feel the confusion and anger in Phoebe's mind, just as she had always been able to feel all her sister's emotions.

In her dream, Steffy cried down the phone, but she could see it all happening anyway. Phoebe getting in the car, angry. Rick driving, refusing to pull over. Phoebe lashing out, pummeling him. Rick trying to stay in control of the vehicle. Phoebe kicking at the accelerator. The car, spinning and careening in those last, fatal, moments.

She saw it all as though she had been there. The screaming metal, the whirling wheels. The sick crunch of steel on road. The screams of her sister and her sister's love.

The sight of Phoebe, her head cradled in Ridge's lap, singing to him the song she had written for his wedding to Brooke. Her sweet angel voice. And then silence.

And then again, as she had relived it a thousand times, and always on this night every year. The feeling. The dreaded feeling that hit Steffy like a knife to the heart.

She was alone. Her twin sister was gone.

*

Steffy woke with a start, as she did every year, on the exact anniversary of the moment when her sister had left her forever. She squirmed in her lush four-poster bed, feeling starched sheets against her legs. She felt the devastation overwhelm her as though it had happened a moment ago.

There were no words for the pain of her loss. This loss of her twin, the other half of herself. The one who had been with her through it all: the desolation of losing their mother, when they thought Taylor dead; their patchy family life; moves from continent to continent, school to school. Her sister, who had been the constant of her life, until the day she had been ripped from her.

And nothing had ever been the same.

Chapter Two

It was two a.m., and Steffy knew sleep would not come back to her easily after that dream. She sat at her desk instead and looked once again at the LA skyline and the blank sketchpad in front of her.

This time, something had shifted. The magic was back.

Liam would laugh at her if she told him it felt as though Phoebe was guiding her hand, trying to show her that life could still be sweet and beautiful. That art and style still had a place in her heart.

She picked up an expensive French charcoal she had been experimenting with in Paris. It flew across the page, and her mind entered that state where the creation was all—that blissful hum where her brain connected with an idea, and all she needed to do was give it free rein. It was as though she were a medium, channeling beauty from another place.

In a couple of hours Steffy had completed three new designs, finally managing to capture the lightness she had seen at the spring shows in Paris, and channel it into something entirely different—a hybrid of the new and old words that was truly unique.

She smiled wryly to herself. At least something good had come from this terrible night.

Finally, at five a.m., she fell into a deep, dreamless sleep, spent by her creative outpouring. And, she was sure, watched by her sister—wherever she was.

*

Steffy contemplated her reflection in the spectacular mirror that covered an entire wall of the master suite in the penthouse. She put her head to one side, wondering for a moment how someone else might see her.

She had worn black, as it seemed fitting for the occasion. A shapely black dress that ended just below the knee, sheer black stockings, black stilettos with a vicious pointed toe, and a short black jacket with a severe collar. The whole effect was serious, almost austere. The black brought out the darkness in her hair, which she had twisted into a sharp little bun at the base of her neck, and the blue of her eyes.

She could see that Liam had been right last night. She did look tired, and even more so this morning, after the night of sleeplessness giving way to the dream. Always the same dream. As she watched her reflection, she could hear her sister's voice, telling her she was too thin, too sad. Telling her it was time to move on. That she needed to find some way to get closure.

Maybe this year, Steffy thought, grabbing a large black tote bag. *Maybe this year I'll find a way to put these demons to rest.* As she reached the doorway, she took one last look back over her shoulder at her reflection. She noticed she was doing it again, unconsciously bringing a hand to her belly, as though to belatedly protect the life she had been unable to save.

A thick surge of disgust engulfed her.

Liam was right. She was not capable of being a parent.

She turned on her heel and headed for the kitchen.

Steffy had sent her housekeeper away for a few days, knowing she would need time alone over this difficult period. She would not be able to face food until after her visit to the cemetery was over, so it didn't matter. Her stomach was churning.

But first, she had another important job to do.

She moved across to the beautiful antique desk and snatched up the three rolled sketches she had completed during the night.

Steffy unrolled one of the sketches, and looked at it again. The purple sheath was like something conjured up from a fairy—one-shouldered and triangular, but gossamer thin. It skimmed the long lines of the model like a whisper, a promise of summer. It was beautiful. Steffy smiled.

Then she noticed what she had done. The model. She had long curly blond hair, an impish grin and a certain look in her eye. Steffy gasped as she realized what she had sketched.

Phoebe.

She quickly unrolled the other sketches. Each of them was a moment of magic. The designs were truly unique, containing something stylish and wild LA had long been missing. And each of them featured her twin sister as the model.

Steffy slowly sat down on one of the elegant leather lounges that marked out the living space. She had planned to drop the sketches in to Forrester Creations before her pilgrimage to the cemetery. But could she do it now? Would others recognize her sister in the sketches?

Did it even matter?

As Steffy considered the questions, her mind spun. Her thoughts flashed from the sketches to her sister to the terrible dreams. And then, as inevitably as breathing, to her argument with Liam last night. She remembered his face, the way he tried to connect with her, reassure her. And she remembered how she had pushed him, willing him to admit what she knew was lying beneath his distance from her. The thing that lay, huge and silent, between them. And then his face as he had lost his temper, thrown the ugly words at her.

Steffy felt herself start to unravel. Spiky tears pricked at the back of her eyes and her breath came hard and fast. But she would not cry.

The thoughts taunted her. All those losses. Liam, the love of her life. Her baby. *Their* baby. The baby she had never known, but had loved so completely for such a short time. And Phoebe. Her twin sister. The other half of her life.

Steffy sat slowly on the couch, breathing deeply and working hard to keep it together. She had felt the tension building, like a gathering storm, in the lead up to this anniversary. And then the fight with Liam, the sleepless night, the catharsis of the early-morning sketching session. It had all pushed her that much closer to the brink.

But she would not cry.

She could cope with this. She was Steffy Forrester. She was strong and brave.

She would *not* cry.

Even when she had lost her baby, she had tried to stay in control. She was the one, after all, who had gotten on that motorbike, knowing she was pregnant, knowing it was dangerous.

Just like Liam said last night.

She had not allowed herself to grieve because she knew she deserved the pain and the punishment. But now it all threatened to come out.

She hugged a cushion and pushed the pain back into the little box she had kept it in for so long. She could do this, she could get through this day, and then return to Paris, and her father, and start over.

Phoebe had always believed in new beginnings, had loved the excitement of a fresh start. Whenever they had started at a new school, a new city, Phoebe had relished the challenge, while Steffy had been slower to settle in. Phoebe was the more intrepid soul. Well, from now on, Steffy would show her sister's memory that she could change, that she could be a better, different woman. She could reinvent and recreate.

Steffy stood and went back to the bedroom for her bag. She closed her eyes, imagining her sister's face as it had been in life, sweet and laughing.

Thank you, Phoebe.

*

Rick Forrester nodded at the young maid as he sipped his coffee, and she retreated quietly. He tried to focus on the words in the newspaper in front of him, but all he could see was the date.

Every year it was the same. As much as he tried to keep busy, plan meetings, be out of town, the date haunted him. He shook his head. He would get nothing done today.

He picked up his cell and punched a number.

His call was answered with Forrester Creations' usual brisk efficiency.

"Cancel my afternoon meetings. I need to be somewhere."

He could hear the surprise in Pam's voice, but she was too professional to ask why. "Yes, sir. Will you need anything?"

"No," Rick snapped. He knew he was being rude, and he tried to soften his voice. "Sorry, Pam, no, thank you. I can handle this one alone."

He stabbed at the end call button, and slammed the phone back on the table, running his fingers through his blond hair, absentmindedly remembering that he needed a haircut.

But the desire to see her kept pulling at him. He pushed aside the Danish pastry he had only nibbled, and stood, taking his wallet from his pocket. He scanned the room quickly, checking that she was not around. He was in enough trouble lately—he didn't need any more.

He sat back down, pulling the little photograph carefully from his wallet and laying it on the breakfast table in front of him.

There she was. Phoebe. Those laughing eyes, that hair that smelled like roses. Sunlight caught in a photograph. He closed his eyes and remembered.

Then the other memories came. The day it had all gone so horribly wrong. Phoebe, so angry with him, jumping in the car, screaming and flailing, hitting out at him. He had been so worried about crashing, and so freaked out by Phoebe's state of mind.

And then the car had rolled and spun, and everything had become a blur of screaming metal and all the darkest fears of the human soul. He had managed to pull himself free and run for help. He would never forget the look on Ridge's face when he had found him. How Ridge had run, desperate with fear and dread, a father terrified for his child.

And then the image that would forever be etched on Rick's brain and his conscience. Ridge cradling Phoebe's head. And Phoebe, using the last of her strength to sing to her father, to let him know that she loved him, accepted him, and understood his demons and his choices.

Rick had watched, knowing he was responsible for this pain, and that there was nothing he could do about it.

He opened his eyes and looked at the little photograph of Phoebe. He had never cried over her—he hadn't allowed himself to. He had no right to it, not with all the suffering he had caused. He'd tried his best to pick up the pieces, to support her family, to be there for Steffy. To atone for his part in all of it. But never had he allowed himself to look fully into the hole that Phoebe had left in his life.

Rick stroked a finger along the graceful jawline of the woman in the photo. He wondered how Steffy was doing today, with her father in Paris. There were so few people who understood what it was like to lose someone you loved. He knew that this was one burden he and Steffy would always share.

Rick brought the photo to his lips, pressing a kiss to it before putting it back in his wallet. He patted the soft leather of the slim billfold and stood to return it to his pants. As he did, he heard the noises of Caroline coming back from her morning ride. She was humming something to herself, and greeting the staff as she made her way into the villa.

Rick couldn't face her right now. He needed his head free and clear for the discussion he knew they had to have, the one he could feel coming. It felt like the coward's way out, but he retreated to the gymnasium when he heard her enter.

He changed quickly into some track pants and an old gray T-shirt he kept there before hoisting himself onto a set of chin-up bars. He needed to burn some energy, release some angst.

He watched himself in the state-of-the-art training mirror as he went through the motions of his usual circuit. He pushed himself to do another press-up and another, going well beyond his usual count, but it was still not enough.

He could see his face in the mirror, grim and determined. Sweat poured from him, but he barely felt the stretch and burn that he sought in his muscles. It was like he wasn't human—nothing could touch him. It was an exorcism.

But it wasn't enough.

Nothing was going to be enough.

Not today.

*

Caroline felt warm and alive. The ride had been with one of her favorite mares, a spirited girl called Star. They had gone right to the outer perimeter of the property, and then Caroline had taken the mare through her paces on the gymkhana circuit. Star had been hot and panting when they had finished, and Caroline had felt her own face flush and her cells sing with exhilaration.

After last night, Caroline had needed the ride.

Rick had tossed and turned in bed. She'd reached out to him at one point and he had thrust her away, babbling incoherently. But it was clear to her that some demon was chasing him.

And she had a horrible feeling it involved another woman.

Why was it she never felt as though she was enough for Rick? Despite their bond, she felt he was always holding something back from her.

As she passed through the foyer, Caroline looked at her reflection in the gold-framed mirror that dominated the space. She was still perfectly groomed, even after the punishing ride. Her soft, slick chignon twisted gracefully at the nape of her neck. Her elegant Ralph Lauren riding shirt set off the raspberry-colored lipstick she had used to highlight her pout. And the tan jodhpurs were just tight enough to tell a story, while still being elegant.

She knew it wouldn't make a bit of difference— Rick seemed to hardly see her right now.

She moved through the living room into the breakfast space, looking for him. She could see the half-eaten Danish and the half-drunk cup of coffee on the breakfast table. She walked carefully to where he had been sitting and softly touched the cup. Still warm. She could smell him in this room, too. That sleepy scent that told her he hadn't been up long. But there was no trace of his tell-tale cologne, so he had not yet dressed for the office. He'd disappeared halfway through his breakfast. Had he heard her coming?

She reached across and rang a little bell on the breakfast table, chewing her lip as she considered the possibilities.

A young maid, the new one, entered the room almost immediately. "Can I help you Ms Spencer?"

Caroline nodded at her. "Mr. Forrester, Rick. Have you seen him?"

The maid frowned a little. She was dark, Spanish-looking, and something about her face reminded Caroline a little of Maya. The thought made her flush. "He was here?"

The maid seemed flustered. "Yes. He was here, only a few moments ago. I'm not sure ..." She put her head to the side. "Sometimes he heads down to the gymnasium after breakfast?"

The girl's pretty uncertainty picked at the sore of Caroline's irritation. "Thank you," she said, in a way she knew sounded dismissive. She mentally chided herself for her rudeness. "Thank you," she said again, quietly. "You may go."

Caroline strode from the breakfast room toward the wide, winding staircase that led down to the gymnasium, tapping her riding crop gently against her leg as she went. She saw him before he saw her.

He was pressing weights on a long, low bench. The barbell seemed to be groaning under the weights stacked at each end of it. Caroline realized she had never seen him lift so much. He seemed to be doing it almost effortlessly, raising and lowering the bar with ease and grace. He was going so fast he looked like a man possessed. She caught sight of his face in the mirror; it was red, but calm. He was a study of intent focus and the thought took hold again.

Possession.

What had driven him mad in his dreams last night? And driven him down here? What was taking him away from her? Was it Maya? Again? She had been sure they had laid that particular demon to rest.

Caroline could not understand his continued fascination with that girl. The whole family seemed to be fooled by her. She was a nothing, an outsider, but she seemed to have something that drew people in.

It was time Caroline found out exactly what was going on inside Rick's head. He had been quiet and distant for weeks now. They needed to talk. And she needed to find out once and for all what he was feeling. It hurt so much to be distant from him.

She wrenched open the glass door into the gym, and Rick swore at the sudden noise, dropping the barbell back into its rests with a loud clang.

"Caroline," he barked. "You startled me." He stood up but didn't move toward her, mopping his face and neck with a thick white towel that had been hanging over the side bar.

"I'm sorry," she said, surprised as ever by the effect his boyish good looks had on her. Like this, dressed only in sweatpants and a drenched T-shirt, his face flushed and his muscles taut, she well remembered what had first drawn her to him.

She wanted to go to him, put her arms around him and kiss him on the mouth, right here in the gym. Her heart rate was still elevated from her ride, and she could see the rapid rise and fall of his chest through the T-shirt. The movement emphasized the broadness of him. She pressed her fingernails into her palms to stop herself from going to him and wrapping her arms around him.

"We have to talk," she said.

*

"What's wrong?" Rick considered the cool, blond beauty standing before him, looking like an ad for polo and the good life. She may have been born with everything, but she was also truly lovely, and she had been so good to him.

But today all he could think about was Phoebe.

Phoebe, who had grown up with everything but managed to stay sweet and sunny and innocent, unaffected by the wealth and power all around her.

His thoughts turned to Maya. Also so different from Caroline. It had been Maya's empathy with the poor and hurting that had drawn her to him.

Caroline was a good person, and beautiful. But he wondered now if they had ever really been the right match for each other. He struggled to understand how they had ever come together. Sure, looking at her he could appreciate the obvious things: her startling good looks; her poise and grace; her kindness; her elegant fashion sense. But there was nothing real between them any more. It was all an illusion. He knew it, because he knew that he was hurting and he didn't want to tell her—she was the last person he would choose to talk to about this, the last person he felt would really understand.

He approached Caroline, feeling a sudden spike of guilt lance his heart. None of this was her fault. She had only loved him, and tried to do the best she knew. They were just ... different.

"Caroline, I ..." Rick said, wondering where to begin.

But she was one step ahead of him. "What happened last night?" Her eyes were bright and glittering and he was sure she could see the distance in his face. Just as he was sure it was hurting her. A wave of self-disgust rose in him.

"Last night?" He'd had wild dreams about the accident again. Always the accident. Dreams where he had done things differently, tried to take a different course, but it always ended up the same. Phoebe lying by the roadside. Rick running wildly, to get help, to find Ridge. And Phoebe dying in her father's arms.

"Was it Maya?" Caroline's mouth was a tight line and her face was closed. He could see she was steeling herself for what he might say. "Was it Maya you were dreaming about?"

"Maya?" This was so far from the truth that he couldn't stop himself from laughing. "No, Caroline," he said, as gently as he could, trying not to communicate his frustration. This was not Caroline's fault. He had no right to feel irritated with her. "This is not about Maya."

As he watched her face relax a little, he realized he owed her an explanation.

She had tried so hard to love him, to be with him and understand him. She deserved to understand.

"It's Phoebe."

Caroline shook her head, mouthing the word he had just said like she was trying to make sense of it. "Phoebe ... Forrester?" Her face was frozen in confusion. "Your ex-fiancée?"

Rick nodded. Hearing the name hurt. It was like all the demons in his head became real as he heard the name on Caroline's lips.

"What about Phoebe?"

He took a breath and put a hand on Caroline's shoulder. "Sit," he said. He ushered her over to a small sitting area at the back of the gym. He sat in an easy chair next to her. "Today is the anniversary of her death," he said, feeling his voice thicken at the words. "The anniversary of the day I—"

Caroline's eyes were wide and waiting.

"The day I killed her."

Caroline's mouth formed a shocked line at his words.

"You're sad," she said finally. "You—you're feeling guilty."

He nodded. "Yes." But he knew it was more than that and he knew he owed it to her to tell her. He took a breath and squared his shoulders.

"Oh my God," she breathed. "You're still in love with her. You're still in love with your dead ex-girlfriend."

Rick swore under his breath. This was not going to be easy. He knew he didn't have a great track record when it came to the women in his life, and he really had done the wrong thing with Caroline in the past. He'd been trying hard to make it work, but he realized now that the reason he had been attracted to Maya, and become so distant from Caroline, was that Caroline simply was not for him.

Rick took Caroline's hands. They felt small and cool in his, which were still warm from the exertions of a moment before.

"I've done a lot of things wrong in my life, Caroline," he said.

She looked up at him, her brown eyes narrow and wary.

"I've spent my life trying to prove something, who I was, what I was. That I was good enough. That I—that I was as good as Ridge, better. He seemed to have everything, even though I was Eric's real son."

Caroline nodded. Rick knew that she understood this about him. She had seen him battling Thomas for control of Forrester Creations, and for her heart. Rick felt his stomach churn as he wondered if she, too, had been all a part of his need to win. It was a hard thing to admit about himself, but he saw now that it could be true.

He dragged in a breath and went on. "In all of that, all that jealousy and fighting to prove myself, I hurt a lot of people. Taylor. Steffy. And, worst of all, Phoebe. I'd made such a mess of everything that she died really believing that I'd never loved her. That I had only become involved with her to hurt Ridge."

He held Caroline's hands firmly. Somehow it was very important that she understand what he was saying. He stood, pushing his chair back brutally and hunting down the right words. Caroline said nothing. She sat like stone and stared at a spot on the wall.

He was hurting her, he could see it. And he wanted to stop.

But he couldn't. Stopping would be the easy thing to do. The thing he had always done before. He needed to make different choices now. And from now on.

"But that wasn't right, Caroline. I *did* love Phoebe. She was so sweet and funny. And, looking back, it was as though she was always destined for sadness. There was something about her that you could never quite grab hold of."

Caroline rose and moved to where Rick was standing, holding out her arms to him. She, of all people, would know how much it was hurting him to admit all of this. Even now, she was being kinder to him than he deserved. But Rick could not step into her arms. He could not give another woman a message he did not mean.

He would not do that any more.

"In all that time, playing with people, I never met anyone like Phoebe. And I killed her as much as if I had pointed a gun at her."

He ran his fingers through his hair, closing his eyes and replaying the scene in his mind. "She was so worked up. I should have pulled over. I just wanted to get to the rehearsal dinner, to get away from her. But I should have known it couldn't go on like that, that we would have an accident."

With the words out, he was still. He finally met Caroline's eyes. "And now, every year, on this day, I think about her. And I think about what I am. Well, that ends today. I'm going to the cemetery. I'm going to talk to her, make my peace with her. And then I'm going to go and see Taylor and Steffy as well. I'm going to ask their forgiveness for all I've done to them, over the years."

Caroline shook her head. She held out her hands to him, as though pleading with an irrational child. "You don't need to do that, Rick. No one blames you—everyone knows that Phoebe was crazy that day. You don't need to open all of this up again—you with Steffy."

Rick saw the fear in her face. This was what she was most concerned about. Rick and Steffy, all over again.

"I do need to, Caroline," he said gently, walking over to her and placing a finger under her chin. He lifted her face to his. "I need you to hear what I'm saying. I know this is hard for you to understand, but I need to be a different man, starting today. That is what all these years have been building to. This is the time for me to change—change everything."

Caroline looked hard into Rick's eyes and he knew in that moment what she was going to ask him. "Including us?"

He wanted to say no; the old Rick would have. The old Rick would have strung her along, made it easy for himself, let her believe he was just having a moment. But he wasn't. This was not about Caroline, and not about Maya. And yet both women, and his inability to commit, to decide between them, were symptoms of a past he had not resolved.

He knew now, after his time at the top at Forrester Creations, that he really was good enough. That he could win hearts and cut deals and do all that he needed to be the man he wanted to be. Now he just had to stop telling lies, to himself and everyone else, and face the future with dignity.

"Yes," he said. "It's over, Caroline. I'm so sorry."

Caroline's hand reached out before he registered what she was going to do. The slap had all the pent-up power of her distress driving it. Rick's cheek stung and his eyes watered as her hand connected.

As soon as she did it, Caroline's hand flew to her mouth. "Oh my God, Rick," she breathed. "I'm sorry, I can't believe I—"

"I deserved that," he said.

Caroline's eyes filled with tears. "Go," she said. "Go see your precious Phoebe, and comfort your precious Forresters." She raised her beautiful chin defiantly, and Rick admired her for gathering herself when she was so obviously in pain. "But don't you think for one moment that you will ever be with someone who understands you the way I do. This is the end, Rick."

He nodded. "Yes, Caroline," he said. "It is." Even with his cheek stinging, the urge to wrap her in his arms and comfort her was almost overwhelming.

But he resisted.

As Caroline turned and walked gracefully from the gym, Rick knew that he should have felt sadness and the stark bite of loneliness that he always so feared about being alone, but instead he felt only a cool wave of relief wash over him.

*

Rick had one more thing to do before he left.

He pulled the small leather case out of his wardrobe, setting it on the bed.

He had changed into a formal black suit, one of his favorite Italian pieces, and a crisp white shirt. He had showered and fixed his hair. He knew, looking in the mirror, that anyone seeing him would see a study of wealth and privilege, the consummate businessman. But the angry red welt on his face would take a couple of days to heal. And it would be a longer time before he would forget the look of dignified pain on Caroline's face as she had stormed out of the gym.

He sat down beside the small leather case, and reached inside for a folded piece of tissue paper. He unfolded it carefully, his fingers feeling thick and clumsy with the delicate thing. As he did, a tiny, pressed daisy chain fell out of the paper and slid onto the cover of the bed.

The sight of it made something cold and dark squeeze his heart. He remembered the day so well, a day from the beginning of his time with Phoebe. When life had been easy and sweet. They had been picnicking and she had made the daisy chain for him, settling it lightly on his hair and then kissing him on his mouth, saying, "My sweet prince."

He had laughed and put it in her hair. It looked beautiful on her, perfect—made her seem even more like the fairy princess she had always brought to mind for him. When they had packed up later, he had grabbed the silly thing. A romantic gesture, perhaps, certainly one unlike him, but he had simply known at the time that he wanted to keep it, to keep that moment alive.

But now it was time to give it back and to say goodbye properly.

He held the little ring of dried flowers carefully in his hands. He could almost hear Phoebe's musical laugh as he looked at it.

Then he carefully wrapped it in the paper and put it back in the leather pouch.

Chapter Three

The warm sun kissed the back of Steffy's hair as she leaned down to consider the bouquets lining the sidewalk. The shop was a riot of color at this time of year. There were roses, of course; scarlet and vermilion and yellow and the most delicate shade of pink. There was something sad about them, their perfect faces straining to the sun, not knowing that they had only such a brief time to enjoy it, that their perfection would soon be dust and memory.

Then there were daisies, always Phoebe's favorite. The sunny round faces peering optimistically at Steffy. Her hand reached for them, brushing one delicate petal, but then the lilies caught her eyes. White, elegant and ghostly. They transported her back to her sister's funeral. She and Rick staring at each other over the casket, caught in a shared bubble of grief and guilt.

Nothing had ever been the same.

The elderly florist who had been hovering in the background surprised Steffy by suddenly appearing above her. "Do you need any help, sweetheart?" Her voice was soft and her eyes kind.

Do I need any help? Steffy thought about the tumult of emotions running though her brain and assailing her heart. Yes, she needed help. She needed her mother. She needed her father. But neither of them could be there for her today. She knew her mother had her own demons, and that today would be difficult for her. She also knew Ridge would be a mess in Paris, reliving the moment his daughter died in his arms, over and over again. She felt her heart trip at the thought that soon she would be back there with him.

"I'm ... I'm okay."

"You don't look okay, dear," the woman said, guiding her over to chairs situated in a little patch of sun under a pretty awning on the pavement. "Sit for a moment and I'll fetch you a glass of water while you collect yourself. There are plenty of gorgeous bouquets here, but I promise you none of them are going anywhere."

Steffy allowed herself to be fussed over. She closed her eyes and enjoyed the quiet moment with the sun on her face.

Before long, the woman was back with a tall glass of water with ice and a tiny slice of lime floating in it. She was wearing a simple calico apron and blue jeans. Her silver hair was pinned in an elegant bun at the base of her neck, not unlike the style Steffy had chosen today, and the woman had lively dark blue eyes that twinkled through the concern etched in the lines around them. She squeezed Steffy's shoulder and looked at her with concern. "You would be surprised, my dear," she said, and Steffy noticed the very slight Southern accent for the first time. "People think flower stores are all about joy and love. Sometimes they're the hardest places to be. You just sit as long as you need to and give me a holler when you're ready to start again."

Steffy nodded and smiled her thanks. The woman's unexpected kindness had touched her, and she felt her eyes beginning to mist over. The woman slipped away, and Steffy could see her making a show of keeping herself busy over near a large stand of greenery.

Steffy was grateful for the moment of peace. She picked up the long, cool glass and ran it over her forehead. She felt suddenly hot and scared. Going to the cemetery was always difficult, but this year it seemed especially so. She took a slow sip, and felt better as the cool liquid settled in her throat. Then she leaned back in the comfortable chair again, to catch her breath and settle her thoughts before returning to the flowers.

She closed her eyes and thought about her plans. She would not think about Phoebe, not yet. There would be plenty of time for that today. For now she would simply sit here and make plans. Firstly, she needed to drop her sketches in to Forrester Creations. She would deliver them to Thomas, and talk to him about what was needed next. It was strange—she'd had such high hopes of launching this new line when she returned from Paris, of starting fresh. But now she knew she was not ready. She would give the sketches to her brother; he would know how to work with them to ensure they shone. She would also let Thomas know that she was taking more time out, and ask him to deal with the administration of it.

And the fallout.

Then she would head to the cemetery, get this over with. Her mind skipped over that part; it would be here soon enough. She didn't need to dwell on it in advance.

There was much to organize. She needed to make some more arrangements to go back to Paris. Sort out the penthouse, let her father know that she was coming back, to spend some proper time with him. That she would stay with him until she was ready to come back. If she was ever ready.

And then there was Liam.

She shut that thought down. Like so much else, she would deal with thinking about Liam later.

After she'd done what she needed to do.

Steffy made a mental to-do list, and felt her sanity and self-possession return. This day was always hard, every year. She just needed to get through it. She decided to sit for one more moment in the sun, eyes closed, before tackling the current task—selecting exactly the right flowers.

*

Rick's breath caught when he saw Steffy sitting in a patch of sun, her dark hair pulled severely back from her face.

She looked thinner than he remembered. And very beautiful.

His hand shook, and his fingers froze on the enormous bunch of daisies he had just selected. Daisies, for Phoebe. And here was her sister, still and serene like a moment frozen in time.

He wasn't ready. He needed to talk to her, needed to make things right with Steffy, and with her mother. But this was not the moment. He had wanted to go to Phoebe first, make his peace, then seek out Steffy and Taylor, see if he could make them understand that he was different. He had changed. And he was sorry.

But now Steffy was here, in the same florist. Surely it was some kind of sign?

He shook his head, realizing that it was logical that Steffy would also choose the florist next to Dayzee's, close to Forrester Creations. She was probably going in to the office to get some work done, and had stopped off here on the way.

But there was something about her face, captured in that yellow shaft of sunlight. He could not take his eyes off her. That bone structure, so delicate and captivating, like Phoebe's, and yet such a different look. She was like a sculpture from a far away time. Even from this distance, Rick could see the full pinkness of Steffy's sultry lips. He tried not to remember what they tasted like—candy and musk. The tiny indentation above her top lip looked like some god had placed his little finger there and created it as a work of art. Like this, her eyes closed, Rick could see the full thickness of her dark lashes, resting lightly in her cheeks.

Yes, she was beautiful.

But he knew more as well. He knew that she was not the person everyone thought to her to be. In the wake of Phoebe's death, they had been drawn together, moths to the flame. Everyone had been outraged, thought it was so wrong. But it hadn't been a game, not that time. It had been the yearning of two souls who recognized something in each other.

Of course, it hadn't worked—could *never* have worked. Not then, with the critical eyes of the world on them, and with all their own grief to manage as well.

Rick knew that Steffy was not the woman the world saw. He knew she could be hard and wild. But he also knew she was soft and caring, and that she yearned to prove herself.

Like him, he thought with a start, wondering why the thought had never occurred to him before.

Then Steffy opened her eyes, and he was rooted to the spot by the power of that blue gaze.

*

"Rick?" Steffy blinked twice, sure she must have napped in this little patch of sunlight after her sleepless night. "Rick?"

It had been some time since she had seen him but as she shook her head to clear it, he was still there. And it was definitely him, Rick Forrester: the last person she needed to see today.

She felt her lip curl as she watched him clutching the huge bunch of flowers, and wondered who he was trying to impress this time. She tried to ignore his boyish beauty. He was wearing a sharp black suit that she recognized as Italian, and it sat well on his muscular frame. She could not remember him looking so fit before she had left for Paris, but the suit showed off his broad shoulders and tapered waist to perfection. His hair was styled boyishly and skimming his collar, and he was very blond too. He must have been making the most of the warm weather, taking the yacht out. His skin was brown, and it showed off his blue eyes.

A red mark stained one cheek.

"Steffy." He nodded. She noticed the haunted look in his eyes, as though he'd seen a ghost. She felt like she'd seen one too.

Was it just because of the significance of this day that she was remembering their time together in such vivid detail? She knew that the world saw Rick as a cad, and she knew better than anyone that he could play the game. She thought about how he had moved from Phoebe, to their mother, to her—all to get to Ridge. The memory made her shudder.

But there was more to him, too.

Or maybe she was just feeling generous because she was tired and emotional.

She sighed. "Sit down," she said, motioning to the chair beside her. "What are you doing here?"

"I'm buying flowers," he said. "For Phoebe."

Steffy felt as though a knife had been driven into the center of her. "Phoebe?" Hearing him say it, seeing him here, knowing what he was doing, made it somehow all so much more real. "Me too," she said, and then her voice broke and she bowed her head. She would not let Rick see her cry. She blinked hard to control the prickly tears that burned behind her eyes. "I'm doing the same. But ..." She willed her voice to stay strong. "I'm still choosing. I just needed to ... take a minute."

"I get it." Something about Rick's face as he said the words gave Steffy pause. She really believed that he did get it. Up close, she could see that he, too, looked tired. And not just more fit than she remembered, but harder too. Older.

Grief had left its mark upon them all.

Steffy's hand went to her stomach again. She saw Rick notice the gesture, and waited for him to change the subject in some smooth segue to lighten the mood. But he didn't.

"Steffy," he said, and this time it was his voice that broke. "I heard your news. I've been wanting to tell you I'm sorry, so sorry for you. But I didn't know you were back. It must have been awful."

Oh my God. Could he really mean the miscarriage? Her baby? She was so used to people not mentioning her baby, the unspoken elephant in the room. Her father. Liam. It felt strange to hear someone say it so simply, and so carefully.

He reached out and touched her hand, very lightly, then grasped it in his. "Steffy."

She couldn't look at him. It was so hard to hold it together, and if he was nice to her, she might dissolve. The last thing she needed today was to throw herself at Rick Forrester.

"Steffy. Are you okay?" Rick turned Steffy's hand over in his, and stroked his thumb lightly across the sensitive skin of her inner wrist.

"No," she said finally, looking into those clear blue eyes. "No, I don't think I am."

He nodded, then stood and shrugged out of his jacket. She watched his broad shoulders ripple through the lush cotton of his white shirt. He sat back down, this time in the chair beside her, and picked up her hand again. "Is this okay?" He looked right into Steffy's eyes. Up close, she could see that the angry red welt on his face was fresh and raw.

He was clearly having a bad day too.

Before she knew what she was doing, she reached up a finger to trace the mark. A nerve jumped in Rick's cheek. "What happened?"

"It was my fault," he began.

Steffy surprised herself by laughing. "You did this to yourself?"

He laughed too, and shook his head. "No, no. It was Caroline."

"Oh." Steffy should have realized. There was a time—perhaps many times—when she could have happily shredded the skin from Rick Forrester's face too. But somehow, that all seemed long ago. Suddenly all that mattered was that Rick was sitting here with her, holding her hand, and knowing that this day mattered to him too; hurt for him too. She appreciated that he had asked about her baby. Not in any way that implied she should somehow be over it, or it shouldn't have mattered, but in a way that seemed to understand that she would feel especially vulnerable about her baby today, when she was remembering the other great loss in her life. "What did you do to her?"

Rick sighed and ran his hands through his hair, leaning forward to put his elbows on his thighs and place his head in his hands. "I—I'm not sure really. Well, I ended it." He smiled at Steffy, a small, self-deprecating smile. "That never goes down too well with women, in my experience."

"Oh," Steffy said again. "No. We don't like it much."

Steffy turned Rick's words over in her mind. She had assumed Rick and Caroline were strong. It just went to show you could never really know the inner workings of other people's lives.

Rick turned to face her, and she felt blown off course by the powerful searchlight of his hot blue stare. He took a deep breath, then blew it out slowly. "Honestly," he said. "I don't think that was the biggest problem for her today."

Steffy nodded. He wanted to tell her something. Something abut this, this bubble they were sitting in together, he wanted to talk. Really talk. She could see it in his face, in the taut lines of his body. "Go on," she said.

"I told her I'd been thinking a lot about Phoebe. About the past. About ... everything."

Rick's eyes darted away from Steffy's at these last words and Steffy was sure he had more to say, but she didn't want to push him.

"We certainly have some past," she said, smiling gently at him.

She closed her eyes again, trying to capture this moment, the sun, the unexpected companionship with this unlikely friend, before she had to get up and do the hardest parts of this day. Then something occurred to her. Somehow she felt sure, in this moment, that he would understand.

"Can I show you something?"

Rick nodded and Steffy reached for her tote. She retrieved the sketches and passed them over to him.

"I did these last night," she said. "I know it sounds kind of crazy but I … I really felt like Phoebe was kind of guiding me." There was something about these sketches. They were part of coming to terms with all that had happened. They were part of this new life she was trying so hard to build. And, weirdly, she could not shake the feeling that this accidental meeting in this florist was part of it too.

Rick looked at the scrolled papers lying on the coffee table in front of them, then nodded at her and leaned forward to pick them up. She felt like a little girl showing someone the pictures she had drawn at preschool, she was so eager to see his reaction. She tried to contain her breathing and sit back as he unrolled the first sketch. His eyes roamed over it.

Time stretched painfully as he looked at the sketch and said nothing. Finally, he lay it down on the coffee table and repeated the procedure with the two remaining designs. Steffy's nerves were at breaking point as she watched him, but she also knew him well enough to know that this was how he operated. He was careful, methodical. He may have done some crazy things out of fear and envy in his private life, but in all matters professional, he was calculated and cool.

As he finished surveying the last sketch, he turned back to Steffy, and she could see that his eyes were wet. "Steffy," he said, taking her hand again. "I don't know what to say." Again, she felt that strong thumb stroke the inner side of her wrist, delicately. She could tell it was meant as a soothing gesture, but it was lighting heat along her veins, making her a little dizzy. She shook her head. What was she thinking?

"Just say *something*," Steffy said.

Rick now took both her hands in his. "The sketches are very powerful, Steffy. The designs alone are ... extraordinary, truly unique. They could spearhead a whole new look for Forrester Creations. I am just so impressed."

"But?" She could hear it in his voice.

Rick picked up her hand and kissed it, and now she knew she wasn't imagining the tears in his eyes. "But they are so much more than that, aren't they? There is so much emotion in those sketches, Steffy, they are more like works of art. And then there's the model."

"Phoebe," Steffy said, bowing her head.

"Phoebe." He dragged in a ragged breath. He pulled her into him, nestling her under one strong arm and wrapping the other around her. "What it must have cost you, taken from you, to create those,

I can't imagine. Just looking at them makes me feel like I've witnessed something private. Tragic."

Steffy nodded. "Something is different this year," she agreed. "It's hard to put into words, Rick. But I feel like ... Every year I go through this, the remembering, the pain. And I've wondered if I'll ever move beyond it. But I know now. Since the baby, I'm not the same person I was. I've grown up, Rick. This year matters more than ever. This year it's time for me to say good-bye to Phoebe properly and move on."

There was more, and she wanted to tell him: the other thing about her baby. For some reason she wanted to tell him. She had not been able to tell Liam, or even her father, but she wanted to tell Rick, right here, in this moment. But something stopped her.

Rick squeezed her tight, and she could not remember ever feeling so completely understood and accepted.

"Let it go, Steffy," he said. "You just need to let it go." He patted her back soothingly. "I believe you when you say that Phoebe was guiding you last night. She was guiding you toward a new beginning. And I want you to know, despite everything that happened, everything I did, I'm here for you too."

At his words, Steffy felt herself melt against his hard, strong chest. Tears pricked her eyes again but she would not cry. But she could let herself lean in and let go with someone she knew understood. And not just that Rick knew and understood about Phoebe. It was more than that. He understood her story, understood about having done things in your life that you are ashamed of, and being marred by them. About wanting to change and grow, and become something better. It felt good to lean against his strength and know that she was accepted—by someone just like her.

As she sat in his embrace, she felt her strength gather. She wasn't sure how long they sat like that. At one point she heard Rick whisper gently to the proprietor, "We're okay, thank you."

After a while, she felt ready to come up for air. She looked at Rick's beautiful white shirt, stained with mascara from the unshed tears trapped on her lashes. "I'm so sorry," she said, trying ineffectually to rub at the spots on the fabric.

"Don't worry about it for a moment, Steffy," Rick said, pulling her back into him. "It's a shirt. It's nothing compared to what you're feeling."

This time, as he pulled her into him, Steffy became aware of Rick as more than a convenient place to gather courage. She felt the long bunch of his muscles under the shirt and inhaled the sweet, salty smell of him. She felt his rough cheek pressing down on the top of her hair and brushing her neck. And with it all came the memories. Rick had been such an attentive, exciting lover.

He had made her feel as though she were the only woman in the world, despite all their history, and all the reasons she should not feel that way. He'd made her feel more secure and loved and special than Liam had ever been able to. With Liam, Hope always lurked in the background, like a dark ghost. Rick had looked at her like she was the only one who could save his soul.

And she remembered it all now as he held her.

She closed her eyes and drank in the sight and smells of him.

And she was sure, really sure, that he was feeling it too. A soft moan escaped his lips and she felt his hot breath on her neck. She could feel his muscles tense in an effort to keep himself in check. She remembered the powerful sensuality that had always defined their relationship. She was sure he was remembering it too, as they sat entwined.

Finally, she forced herself to pull away. "Rick, I—thank you." She smiled into those dark blue eyes that seemed to burn a hole right through her. "I really needed a hug today." She was talking too fast, trying to make light of it, trying to dismiss what had just passed between them.

But he smiled back at her, his eyes frank and full of understanding. "Any time, Steffy." He stood up and held out a hand to her. "Now, I have my flowers. How about if I come and help you choose yours?"

*

It hadn't seemed right to blurt out what he wanted from her when she had clearly been so distressed. He'd wanted to tell her that he was sorry for all he had done. And that he wanted absolution.

But it wasn't until he had seen her that he had really connected with how she must be feeling today.

He felt like a fool.

This day wasn't just about him. It wasn't his place to be throwing his weight around, making demands for forgiveness. No, he needed to earn it. Steffy needed someone today. Her father was in Paris. And her mother was—well, Taylor was dealing with her own issues. He wanted to ask whether Steffy had any support today, but it was clear from the way she had collapsed on him that he was it. She was all alone, as alone as he felt right now.

And then there was the other confusing thing: that hug, that he had truly intended as a way to offer comfort and solace, had ended up something else entirely. Or had that just been his overactive imagination, and some echo of their history? All he knew was that as he held her, he'd felt something blossom between them. The familiar scents of her: that Japanese perfume she adored; the fragrant shampoo she used on her hair. And the heady, sweet smell of her skin. It had all worked its way into his brain—and through it, shooting a message straight to his heart.

And somewhere much lower.

He had tried to stop himself becoming aware of her as a woman, but it had been impossible. He shook his head to clear the unwelcome thoughts. He knew now what he needed to do. If he truly wanted to change, if he truly wanted to earn her forgiveness, and make things right with Phoebe's memory, he needed to support Steffy today.

He smiled at her as they considered the stand of roses. "What does mademoiselle like?" He knew his French accent wasn't bad, but she wrinkled her nose cutely.

"These, I think," she said, touching the soft petals of the pale yellow roses gently. "Something about them reminds me of her."

He nodded. "I agree." He motioned to the older woman behind the counter and passed her a bill as she made her way over. "Can we have these, please?"

"A perfect choice, sir," she said, smiling at them both. "Perfect."

As she bustled away to wrap them up, Rick steeled himself.

"Steffy," he began. "I wonder if you might like to come with me to the cemetery today. I mean, I understand if Liam—"

Steffy cut him off. "No," she said quickly. "Liam won't be coming with me." She reached up again and touched the mark on the side of his face. "You aren't the only one who said some goodbyes lately, Rick."

Rick cursed himself for the thrill of pleasure that raced through him at her words. No Liam. Once it would have caused him pleasure just to know that he had one over that little upstart, but now it was more than that. He was glad that he could be here, with Steffy, and give something to her, rather than take. Some comfort, some support. He knew that he understood better than Liam, perhaps better than anyone, what Steffy was going through today.

But Steffy still wasn't saying yes. "Why, Rick? Why do you want to come?" Her eyes were narrowed, and for the first time she seemed to remember a little of their other history, the dark past that bound them all together. Rick saw the wariness and suspicion creep into those hot blue eyes.

"Because you need someone," Rick said. "And I need someone too. Because today is hard for both of us. For some reason, this year is different. Let me drive you. I promise you can have all the alone time you need once we're there. I just ... I just don't want you to be by yourself today, Steffy."

She smiled at him, and slipped a hand into his. He felt warm and happy as she did it.

"I don't want to be by myself either," she said.

"Good," he said, smiling down at her. "But we have to find a home for those sketches first." He turned and began walking toward the Forrester Creations offices.

Steffy hesitated. "I thought—"

"What is it? You don't want to go into work today?"

"No, yes, I mean—It's just—I had wanted to give these to Thomas to work with."

Rick felt the usual animosity and competitiveness flare in his blood as she said it. The sketches were remarkable. He had not been exaggerating when he had said he felt they could truly reshape the way Forrester Creations approached the season.

Then he looked at Steffy's face. He took in the dark shadows bruising the delicate skin under her eyes. He closed his own eyes and brought the sketches to his mind. Their other-worldly colors, the inspired designs. And, most of all, Phoebe's face.

They belonged to Steffy. And to Phoebe. It was right that their brother should shepherd these new ideas through development.

This was not about Rick, or his ego.

It was time to grow up. To show that he could be bigger than his rivalry with Thomas.

He nodded. "Great idea. Let's go and see him together."

Chapter Four

Steffy's palms were clammy as she walked through the corridors of Forrester Creations with Rick, thinking about what Thomas would make of her designs. She hoped he would understand what she had created with the sketches, and that they would mean as much to him. This was part of what she needed to do to honor Phoebe's memory and to carve out something new for herself.

But what if she saw Eric?

She had avoided her grandfather since her return. There was so much to explain, and she wasn't sure if she could get through it without breaking down. And then, of course, he would want her to stay. She gripped the bag with the sketches carefully in her hands. Especially if he saw these. Eric Forrester was nothing if not shrewd. He would see the value of this new idea, and demand that Steffy stay to see it through.

But Steffy knew that it was not Forrester Creations, LA, and all the madness of their family that she needed right now. She needed some time and space while she worked through the next steps. She needed Paris. She needed her father.

And right now, she needed Rick. For some reason, he was her lifeline in this awful day.

The world was a fuzzy bubble, the expensive art on the walls one long blur of color and glass. Rick was guiding her through the hallways carefully, one hand solicitously at her back. Steffy could feel the warm pressure there, and the heat rising from his body, even through his jacket. His presence was partly comforting, and partly disconcerting. Something about his hand at her back felt so right, and she had to keep reminding herself that he was just taking care of her; this wasn't like it had been before. They were not together, they were just leaning on each other today. She needed someone. And it seemed perhaps he did too.

Rick stopped her with a gentle pressure on the small of her back and Steffy realized they were outside the door of his office suite. He looked down at her, and his blue eyes were kind. "I've been thinking about what I said before, Steffy," he said. "And I think you should go and see Thomas yourself. I'm not sure I'm his favorite person."

Steffy nodded, knowing it was true but feeling suddenly bereft.

"I'll wait here," Rick said. "Come back when you're ready and I'll bring the car around so we can go together."

Steffy was touched by his concern, and impressed that he was not insisting on coming with her to see Thomas. Like everyone else, Thomas didn't know she was back. Steffy had begged her father not to tell anyone she was coming home, to give her some space with Liam. And then when Liam had left, she'd asked him to keep quiet as well. So Thomas would be surprised to see her. He might even be a little offended that she hadn't contacted him. She had planned to, but after the problems with Liam, she just needed some time to herself.

She wondered how Thomas was doing today. No doubt the anniversary would be hard for him too. She shut her eyes, wondering if he would insist on accompanying her to the cemetery.

Everything in her rejected the idea. This day was so hard every year, but this year it was harder than normal. It was so personal. She wanted to tell Phoebe about the baby and about Liam and she didn't have it in her to support someone else as she did. Rick had been clear that he would be there to help her. She couldn't prop someone else up when she felt like she was falling apart herself.

As all these thoughts did battle in her head, she felt herself sway on the spot in Rick's doorway.

"Steffy!" He was at her side in an instant and he had an arm around her neck and another around her waist in seconds. He picked her up as though she weighed no more than her tote bag and very gently carried her over to the large chesterfield by the window in his office. She should protest, she should complain, but as she considered the ideas, the world grew even fuzzier, and she felt blackness swim in her vision. She felt warm and safe in the cocoon of his solid arms and she wondered vaguely if she was going to pass out. The world began to tilt and go fuzzy, and her stomach turned watery. She clung to the reassuring feeling of Rick's warm body holding her tightly.

Rick laid her carefully on the couch, and kneeled beside her. "Steffy, listen to me." She still felt floaty but tried to focus on his voice. "Have you eaten anything today?"

Steffy tried to remember. Had she? "No," she mumbled, having a hard time connecting the dots.

Rick grunted. "Hmm. And I'm sure you didn't get much sleep either. You're exhausted, and so thin. And it hasn't been very long since you—since you lost the baby. I think we need to get you a doctor."

At Rick's words, Steffy's brain clicked back into gear. "No." She reached for his arm and grabbed a handful of starched cotton shirt. "No, Rick, please don't. I couldn't bear it. Not a doctor. I ..." She closed her eyes, remembering all those white coats buzzing around when her heart was breaking after losing her baby. She imagined all the drama that would ensue if an ambulance was called to Forrester Creations. Everyone would know of it in moments. She didn't need the scrutiny today.

But Rick was already shaking his head. "No, Steffy, I want to get you looked at. You—"

Steffy interrupted him again, shaking her head to try to clear it. "Honestly, Rick, I just need a bite to eat. Or something to drink. Maybe some orange juice?"

"Orange juice?" Rick's voice had become louder, and he was looking at her with irritation and something else she couldn't quite work out. "It's not orange juice you need. It's rest, and food, and maybe some medical attention."

As he spoke, his brows drawn down in consternation, Steffy realized he was very, very worried about her. He confirmed it the next moment.

"God, Steffy, I thought you were going to collapse a moment ago. You scared the life out of me."

"I'm sorry." She smiled at him, trying hard to reassure him that it was a momentary lapse and that she was really fine. "I just … I guess I really should have eaten something this morning."

He frowned at her, then his face cleared as he seemed to decide something. He stood up quickly. "Okay, then. No doctors. For now." He said the last words in a gruff voice that suggested he was reserving his judgment about whether he would call a doctor or not. "But only if you agree to lie here a little while and rest before you go to see Thomas. I'll have Pam order you some food, and I'm choosing it. No orange juice, okay?"

She smiled at him again. "Okay."

"And no complaining."

She raised an eyebrow at him. "Don't push your luck."

*

Rick looked down at the beautiful woman on his chesterfield. The antique piece of furniture always pleased his eye. He relished its solid lines and elegant design and often stared at it when he was musing over a troubling problem, or thinking through a new course of action. It soothed him. But it had never looked as appealing as it did today, with Steffy Forrester lying on it.

He crouched down beside her again, the urge to comfort and protect her rising in him. But he had no right to feel that. She was not his, and they both had complicated issues they were working through today.

He reminded himself again: today he was here for her.

He picked up a soft, loose curl and tucked it behind her ear. Her eyes fluttered open and he was momentarily caught in their sweet web.

He felt a little guilty, like a schoolboy caught staring. "Steffy, I—"

"Rick!" The voice from the doorway caught him off guard, and he stood quickly, putting the hand that had touched that soft curl behind his back like it had been in the proverbial cookie jar.

Caroline had changed from her riding clothes to an elegant gray suit with a ruffled fuchsia blouse underneath. Her hair was loose and silky, swinging about her shoulders. She looked perfectly groomed but very sad. High pink spots lit both her cheeks, and her eyes were rimmed with red.

He looked quickly over at Steffy, who was trying to pull herself up from the couch. She was very pale.

"I came to say sorry," Caroline said. "For this morning. For—" She motioned to his cheek, and as she did, he could almost feel the bruise throb where she had slapped him. Then she glanced at Steffy. "But I can see you've already moved on."

"Hi, Caroline," Rick said, moving over to her and guiding her with his body out of his office. The last thing Steffy needed was to be subjected to a scene between him and Caroline. "Steffy is having a rest in my office. She—"

"I didn't even know she was back," Caroline said. "I thought she was in Paris with her father. And where's Liam? Why isn't he here to be the knight in shining armor?"

"It's complicated," Rick said, looking for the right words to shield Steffy's secrets and manage Caroline's sadness with minimum pain for all.

"Oh, it always is." Caroline pushed past Rick to where Steffy was lying on the chesterfield. "With you Forresters."

Rick hurried to join her, but Caroline was already standing over Steffy, who was blinking up at her in confusion.

"I'm sorry, Caroline." Steffy slurred. "I don't know what I've—"

"Please don't 'Sorry, Caroline' me," Caroline said, as Steffy lifted herself up on the chesterfield. Caroline blinked back tears as she stood over Steffy, and Rick could hear that she was speaking from the hurt of their conversation this morning. This was not like Caroline, and his heart ached for her as she stood over Steffy, pink-cheeked and furious. "The poor, tragic Forrester women." Her voice broke. "Why? Why can't you all just be happy with what you've got, with *everything* you've got…?" Caroline brought her hands together in a gesture of supplication. "Why do you all have to come between Rick and me? Everything would be okay, we could work things out, if only you'd leave us alone."

"That's enough." Rick grasped Caroline's upper arm and steered her out of his office as quickly and gently as he could. It was difficult, because he didn't feel like being gentle any more;

he felt like calling security and having Caroline thrown out of his office. He knew she was hurting, he understood that, but he had tried to be as clear as possible this morning. And now Steffy was unwell, and he needed to keep Caroline's sadness and growing anger away from her. He turned back to Steffy as he propelled Caroline through his door once more. "Lie down, Steffy," he said. "I'll be back shortly."

He shut the door carefully behind them, and spun Caroline toward him, still holding her arm. "Please listen, Caroline. I don't want to hurt you. Ever. But I tried to explain this morning. I tried being careful with you. But obviously you need to hear this one way only. It is over between us. I'm happy to talk to you some more when it's the right time." He took a breath. "But that time is not now. Please go. And please, *please*, leave Steffy out of this. What happened between you and me is not about Steffy."

*

The mid-afternoon sun hurt Steffy's eyes and she slipped on a pair of oversized sunglasses she'd picked up on the Riviera. Rick was waiting back in the car. He had suggested she go first and have some time with Phoebe, and Steffy had appreciated the gesture more than she could say. She could see him from where she was standing. He had one door open as he waited, parked beneath a stand of trees, and was working on his iPad. One leg was propped up on the door, and he'd shrugged out of his jacket and removed his tie in the afternoon heat. His white shirt was open.

The cemetery stood high on a hill, with sweeping views to Santa Monica and the ocean beyond. Trees and shrubs grew wild, and the headstones were placed in distinct areas. The Forrester family plot stood among a stand of pine trees. Phoebe would have loved it here.

Her sister's grave was awash with color and perfect, just as Steffy remembered it. As she crouched to lay the yellow roses by the gravestone, she caught sight of an enormous bunch of tropical flowers she knew could only have come from one person. She glanced at the card quickly.

My darling girl. Forever. Your loving mother.

As Steffy pressed her eyes shut, she felt the tears that she had been battling all day begin to slide under her lids. She gently touched another bouquet. White gardenias, wrapped in a beautiful crimson ribbon. She rubbed one of the gardenias gently, feeling the softness of the petals. The gilt-edged card just read: *Dad*. Steffy had never discussed Phoebe with her father—it was an unspoken agreement between them. Some things were too painful to discuss, and Steffy knew that her father had experienced the worst of that day—holding Phoebe as she had passed away.

Everything about the day screamed of life. The trees and shrubs burst with color. A riot of birds squawked from the pine trees around her. The sun beat down on them, warm and vibrant. She could smell the heady, nostalgic aroma of fresh cut grass. Puffy clouds skittered overhead like they were chasing each other in a game of tag.

But Phoebe was dead.

Steffy thought about the sketches her sister had guided her to the night before. Sure, they had been partly inspired by Steffy's time at the shows in Paris, but there was something else about them—something so colorful and otherworldly—that seemed also to be a celebration of life. Steffy wondered if this was what Phoebe was trying to tell her.

Life was here, all around her, despite the loss of her baby.

Despite the loss of Liam, the love of her life.

Despite the loss of her sister, the other part of her soul.

As she considered the thought, she knew it was true. The last six years had been like a hiatus, holding her breath, waiting to feel whole again. But as Steffy stood in front of her sister's grave, her beautiful sister who would never feel the sun on her shoulders again, she realized it was an indulgence. She had to live, because life had been given to her, a perfect gift. She realized she had to make every moment count, for all the moments Phoebe would never have.

Steffy kneeled on the grass. "I promise," she said. "I promise that from now on, things will be different. I'm not that person any more. The one who hurt you. The one who was so selfish, and so reckless. I had a baby, Phoebe. A little baby. But I lost it, because of my own selfishness and stupidity. And I've lost Liam as well."

She leaned forward and kissed her sister's head-stone. It felt rough and warm against her lips, and even this seemed like a message. She was alive.

"But no more. I am going to live well, and fully. I am going to live a beautiful life, for both of us." Steffy reached across and adjusted the roses where she had laid them, making sure they were beside the bouquets from her mother and father. As she did, she thought about the flowers Liam had brought her when she had lost her baby: perfect pink camellias. And she remembered his face when she had told him. The devastation there.

Perhaps she had been too harsh to judge him for what he was feeling. It was natural that he would look for someone to blame—wasn't blame one of the stages of grief? And she knew he didn't need to look too far. She was rocked by a sudden and overwhelming need to connect with Liam, to tell him that she understood his sadness.

She had been so angry at him for not being there for her.

But had she really been there for him?

Perhaps making things right with Liam was all part of growing up, learning to embrace life. Not so they would be together again. Perhaps that would happen, perhaps it would not. But because it was the right thing to do. He had lost something too.

She stood up again, and adjusted her clothes. "Goodbye, darling Phoebe. Until next year."

As she began the slow walk up to the car, she saw Rick notice her and step out of the car to walk toward her. They met halfway.

"Are you okay?" His eyes were a very dark blue, and she noticed he had put his jacket back on for his visit with Phoebe. He was standing close to her with the bunch of daisies and a strange, desiccated daisy chain in his hands. He was so close she could hear his breaths. He reached out and touched her gently on the shoulder, rubbing it a little with his hand.

She considered the question, her head on the side. "Yes," she said, nodding. "I think so. I'm—I'm still feeling a bit fragile, but I feel a lot better." She motioned to the daisy chain. "What's that?"

He smiled sadly at her. "Closure." Then he squeezed her shoulder again and motioned toward Phoebe's headstone. "I'll just take a few minutes," he said. "Why don't you wait in the car?" He smiled at her, and she smiled back.

"Rick." She held out a hand to touch his upper arm as he went past her.

He looked back at her, his eyes creasing in concern. "Do you need me to stay with you?"

"No, it's not that." She lowered her eyes, worrying that it would sound trite. But she meant it more than she had meant anything she'd said to a man in a very long time. "Thank you," she whispered. "Thank you for being here today."

Rick wrapped his hand around her fingers where they rested on his arm. "No, Steffy," he said. "Thank you. Thanks for everything. For letting me come with you today. For the sketches. For sharing how you felt with me. And for not telling me to go to hell, and never come back, as you had every right to."

She nodded at him. "We've both done things we regret," she said. Then she swept her eyes down the hill to the headstone. "Go be with Phoebe."

*

Steffy paced back and forth out the front of the little French bistro, waiting for her call to connect. The bistro was the perfect place to regroup after the emotional turmoil of the cemetery. Rick had suggested they stop for a drink and some food, and Steffy knew food was a good idea after feeling faint earlier in the day.

But first, she had to speak to Liam. She had to make it right with him, like she had decided at Phoebe's graveside.

She'd told Rick she needed to make a couple of calls.

He'd grinned at her. "Okay, but if you're not there to order, I'm making yours a cheeseburger with everything."

She'd laughed, pointing at the rustic little sign near the entry: Le Chat Noir. "I don't think this is that kind of place," she said. But she didn't doubt that he would do it. He had been looking at her with protective concern ever since her spell in his office. She would not put it past him to order her an enormous meal, and hand feed it to her.

As Rick had retreated, she'd tapped Liam's image on her smartphone and held it to her ear, her fingers shaking.

The signal bleated in her ear and she felt her heart rage in her chest. Why was she so nervous? Her mind replayed the scene the night before.

Finally, the familiar message greeted her. "Hi. You've reached Liam. You know the drill." His voice was so soft and authoritative, so sweetly familiar, that she felt tears spring to her eyes as she listened to the message. She blinked them back as she almost lost the ability to leave a message of her own. She took a deep breath. A new day. A fresh start.

"Liam, it's Steffy. I wanted to talk to you. To say sorry, for last night. Maybe you can call me when you have time? I'm near the cemetery, at a little French place—" Her voice broke on the word, but she ploughed on, swallowing hard.

"I'm taking some time, having a rest, but I'll be back at the apartment later tonight. Perhaps you can call me then?"

As she hit the end call button, Steffy felt a lightness fill her. Yes, it was right that she connect with Liam, so that things did not end badly between them. Life was short, and you never knew what might be around the corner. She and Rick knew that only too well. Neither of them would ever have imagined the last time they had seen Phoebe that they would never see her again.

She stuffed the cell back in her tote and walked back into the bar, seeing Rick sitting at a corner booth, sipping a red wine and looking out the window.

This felt right too.

*

Rick was enjoying watching Steffy eat; it was as though she was making up for lost time. They had started with wine and appetizers—some escargot and bread. But they'd now been sitting and talking for over an hour, and she was now attacking a bowl of aromatic vichyssoise with gusto. It wasn't a cheeseburger, but it sure looked like it was hitting all the right spots.

"What are you grinning at?" Steffy raised an eyebrow at him as she wiped the corner of her mouth delicately with a starched white napkin.

By tacit agreement, they hadn't discussed Phoebe. Not yet. Rick wanted Steffy to have a moment to relax, after all she had been through. He knew better than most that there were few relaxed hours when you were a Forrester, let alone on day like today. So he asked her about her time in Paris—what she had seen, her impressions of the shows, the food, the people. He had forgotten what a good storyteller she was.

Relaxing on her second glass of wine, Steffy seemed to come alive talking about the country. "Monsieur Duchamps and his wife were the care-takers of the little hotel Dad set up base in. They're so sweet, treated me like their granddaughter." She paused, her soup spoon en route to her mouth. "Maybe a little too much, you know?"

He shook his head, wanting her to continue. He just liked listening to her. "No. How do you mean?"

"Well ..." She wiped her mouth delicately with the napkin. "They couldn't cope that I wasn't there with some man. They made it their life mission to find me a good French boy. Apparently I was—" Steffy pursed her lips and affected a very decent French accent, "'—a beautiful girl badly in need of a French lover.'" She rolled the last R authentically. "They proceeded to trail a pro-cession of eligible young men through the bar, hoping to catch my interest. It was sweet." She took another sip of her soup. "Until the day they introduced me to one particularly charming comte who tried to lure me back to his castle in the French countryside. When he realized I wasn't so keen, he was outraged. He said: 'Mon Dieu, don't you know who I am?'" She threw her head back and laughed and Rick found himself greedily drinking in the sight of her long white neck. She looked good when she was relaxed like this.

She looked good any old way.

"Did you tell him who *you* were?" Rick didn't want this to stop. Not her laughter, not the story, not the day.

"You know," Steffy said, finally sighing and pushing her soup bowl away. "I really don't think it would have mattered. The French just aren't that impressed by Americans, whatever they've done. I'm pretty sure his castle would have trumped Forrester Creations any day. At least in his own mind."

As they laughed over the anecdote, Rick leaned forward and grasped Steffy's hands. "She would have loved to see you laughing like this."

There was a moment of silence between them. They both knew what he was doing—it was time to discuss the elephant in the room. But he didn't want to press her. "It's okay, Steffy," he said, reaching over to stroke one of her hands. "We don't have to talk about Phoebe. Not if you don't want to. We have all the time in the world. I'm not going anywhere."

She nodded at him. "How was it?" She squeezed his hand as she said the words. "How was it for you today, at the cemetery?"

Rick hadn't expected this. He had wanted to be there for her, to give her some support. Let her talk. He had carefully tucked away his own grief as he had walked back from Phoebe's grave after giving her the perfect daisy chain.

He looked at her carefully. "It was … confronting," he said. "I'm not like you, Steffy. Maybe not as strong as you. Usually, I avoid this day. I keep busy, or I get drunk." He gave a small smile. "Often both."

She nodded, and squeezed his hands again. "But this time I decided it was going to be different. I was going to be different. I was going to be better."

"Tell me," she said, widening her eyes to encourage him to continue.

He wasn't sure how much to tell her. Would she understand? But everything about this day—seeing her at the florist, going to the grave with her—it was like it was all building to this. The bar was dark and intimate. He could see that she had relaxed from the place she had been earlier in the morning. Her cheeks were rosy and the dark shadows under eyes had faded a little.

"I always felt like I had no right to grieve." He shrugged. "Because I was responsible. This year I decided I needed to. To move on, to get better.

To grow up, I guess. I knew I'd never be able to give myself properly to anyone else, or live the life Phoebe would have wanted me to live, if I kept myself wrapped up in this armor of self-hatred and guilt." He looked down at his hands in hers. "I guess it was just time." He didn't want to look up at her, lest he see recrimination in her eyes. Or worse, see that he pricked her own grief with his indulgent outpouring.

But when he looked at her, he saw only warmth and understanding in her eyes. And maybe something else.

Recognition?

Slowly, she stood from her seat and walked to where Rick was sitting. She slid wordlessly in next to him, then reached up her arms and wrapped him in them. He was enveloped in the candy-sweet warmth of her.

"I get it, Rick," she whispered in his ear. "I can honestly tell you that I really do get it."

She pulled away from him, and Rick felt himself sigh at the loss of her. But she stayed close, and began speaking into her drink. "I wanted to call her Phoebe," she said.

At first, Rick was confused. Then he saw that gesture, her tell. Her hand went to her stomach, and she could not meet his eyes. Of course, the baby.

Steffy went on. "If she was a girl, I'd planned to call her Phoebe," she said. "But I didn't know that of course ..." Rick felt his chest constrict at the raw grief in her voice. "I still don't know. They couldn't tell me."

Rick went to put his arm around her again, but she shook it off. He knew that she was not rejecting his offer of comfort. He could feel from her gaze, directed at her glass, and from the set lines of her shoulders, that this was something she had to get out. "I loved my baby, you know. From the moment I knew about it, I loved it. But I was too foolish, too—" Her voice broke.

"Steffy." He couldn't bear it. "You don't need to do this."

"No," she said, shaking her head. "I do. I was too selfish to protect my baby properly, like a mother should. I got on that motorbike and it died. And you know what?"

Finally, she looked up at Rick and he could see that her eyes were wet with tears. He shook his head. "No," he said. "What?"

"I never let myself cry for my baby. Not really. Just like you never let yourself cry for Phoebe." She shrugged, looking down at her glass again and swirling the fine merlot around and around. "I cried out of bitterness, and I cried out of self-recrimination and I cried out of self-pity, and self-hatred." She looked up at him again, and now the tears were coursing down her pink cheeks. "But it was only today, at that grave, that I really felt sorry for me. And for my baby. For what we lost in each other. I lost my baby. And I also lost the chance to ever, *ever* be a mother."

Rick felt his sharp intake of breath as she said it. He hadn't realized. But he didn't say anything, because he could tell she wasn't finished.

"I know I've done bad things. I know I probably deserve only bad things. But I never, ever dreamed that I deserved that." The words seemed dragged from the deepest, darkest place in her. Her voice was low and ragged, and her face was creased with pain.

He took her hands from around the wineglass, very gently, feeling like she might break. He turned her toward him in the wide booth seat. She was still looking down at their hands, so he put one finger under her chin and lifted it up so she would meet his eyes.

"No," he said. "No you did not, Steffy. You did not deserve any of it. And if I could take it away for you, I would."

As he said the words, he enfolded her in his arms again, bringing her very close to him, almost pulling her into his lap. He wanted to shield and comfort her. There was something primal and terrifying about the force of his need to make it all okay for her.

He felt her melt against him.

Chapter Five

Steffy inhaled deeply as she leaned against Rick's shirt. He'd changed out of the one ruined by her mascara and unshed tears and he smelled like the outdoors, as he always had—the sea, salt and a faint trace of earthiness. A very light cologne overlaid the other scents and Steffy found herself breathing deeply, enjoying the comforting but sensual fragrances.

Rick's arms were tight and warm around her. For the first time in a long time, her muscles completely relaxed. It had been an exhausting day and one she was almost sure she could not have survived without Rick. His quiet, solid presence had held and comforted her. Without it, she was not sure she could have even made it to the cemetery.

And now this.

The little bistro was the perfect choice—quaint and dark, intimate without being romantic. The dark wood paneling and low ceilings reminded her of a place she had stopped with her father when he had insisted they take a drive to the Loire Valley one weekend.

As she felt herself melt against Rick, something shifted between them. Again. His arms, which had been firm but relaxed, tensed a little, and he shifted in his seat. She felt his nose press down lightly into her hair. He picked up one long, loose curl and wrapped it around his finger, seeming to enjoy the silky length of it. The soft tug on her scalp galvanized her senses, awakening her skin and lighting a trail down her neck to her spine.

This sweet, comforting hug seemed to be turning into something else entirely, and while Steffy was pretty sure she should stop it in its tracks, her body didn't seem to agree. Ten more seconds, she promised herself.

But it was ten seconds too long. Because as she leaned against the hard length of the man who had been caring for her all day, a familiar voice broke into her reverie.

"Steffy!"

She sprang from Rick's arms as though Liam had caught her in his bed, not his embrace.

Liam looked furious and wild. His well-cut gray suit was askew, his tie flipped causally over one shoulder. Steffy registered dark shadows under his eyes and tense lines around his mouth. His gaze was thunderous, looking from Steffy to Rick as though they were teenagers and he was the father who had discovered them necking in the back of a car.

"Liam?" Steffy's brain hurried to catch up. "Why are you here? How did you know where I—"

"Feeling guilty?" Liam's voice could have sliced through diamond. If Steffy thought he had been upset with her the night before, it was nothing on the freeze he was laying down now. He stood close to the edge of the booth and Steffy wriggled out to stand in front of him. Rick followed, his hands held up in front of him in a calming gesture.

"Liam," Rick said. "This is not what you're thinking."

Liam stepped toward Rick, his face closed and his brown eyes darkening almost to black. "Oh, and you'd know all about what I'm thinking, wouldn't you, Rick?"

Steffy watched Liam and Rick standing close to each other. Rick, who had been so careful and gentle with Steffy all day, was suddenly poised for action. She had thought this morning that he seemed more powerfully built than she had remembered, and the thought came to her again as she watched him, his fists bunched and his body braced in the stance of a boxer.

Steffy's head swam. No. This was all wrong. She did not need this. Not today. It was ridiculous. She and Rick had been doing nothing wrong. Okay, she had felt the subtle shift between them as Rick hugged her, but thoughts were not deeds. Rick had been giving her a comforting hug. He knew better than anyone what she had been through today. And she had gripped him like a lifeline. She was not prepared to feel bad about that now, not when Liam had so continuously refused to acknowledge her pain, or even her right to grieve. He had been pretty clear last night that things were over between them. Who was he to come here now and start scowling and growling at them both?

Steffy carefully inserted her body between the two men, feeling the air thicken around her. She faced Liam.

Liam's brown eyes shifted from narrow and dark to wide and uncertain. That little-boy-lost look that she knew so well and loved so much. When he was like this, there was a vulnerability to him that touched something inside her. "Why? Why did you ask Rick to come to the cemetery with you? I would have come. You only had to ask."

Steffy's head swam, and the tight pull of a headache drilled at the back of her neck. She swallowed hard on the lump that rose like a stone in her throat. "I don't want to have to ask," she whispered.

And she realized it was true. She had never consciously thought that she wanted Liam to talk to her about her sister, and about what this day did to her every year. But after today, after Rick's comfort and concern, she knew she had been missing something. It felt good to have someone ask about her, care about her, wonder if she was okay on this awful day.

When she saw Liam's eyes narrow again, she rushed to fill the silence. "I mean, I didn't plan it." She stepped back and turned to Rick, imploring him with her eyes. "We didn't plan it. I just ran into him, at the florist. It's something we share. It's—"

Liam held up a hand. "Well, that's Rick, isn't it?' he scoffed. 'Mr. Convenience. Always in the right place at the right time. *A swell guy*." Liam's mouth twisted into a wry line.

"Liam!" Steffy was shocked by the bitterness in Liam's voice. She wondered what else this was about. Last night, they had both been clear that things were over between them. He had been furious with her, and she with him. Why did he think he now had rights to her? And why was he so incensed with Rick?

"Don't 'Liam' me," he growled, and she could feel his fury growing. "I suppose it was just convenient to stop off at this nice little place on the way back. Have a drink and a bite to eat to soothe your souls after a hard day."

Rick stepped forward, looking like he had had just about enough of Liam's accusations.

"She's tired, Liam," he said, putting a hand on Steffy's arm. "Look at her. Can't you see? All she's been through in the last few months. And then today."

A low growl slid from Liam's mouth. "Don't talk to me about all she's been through, Forrester," he said. "I've been through it with her. We went through it, together. And don't think I don't know what you're doing, what this is all about. You've never been crazy about my personal life. And my choices." He said the last word slowly and deliberately.

Steffy looked at Liam carefully, shaking her head as she tried to process what he was saying.

"You didn't much like it when Hope and I were happy either," Liam said, making sure Rick knew what he meant. "You had to be the disapproving brother. And now Steffy. Once again, it's as though you're determined to get in my way."

Steffy felt Rick's hand tighten on her arm and the world seemed to slow down. The small, dark bar suddenly seemed very close. The lights swam in her vision.

Oh my God. Hope.

This was all about *Hope*.

And Liam. Liam not getting what he wanted. Liam being thwarted. It wasn't about her at all. Not about wanting her. Not about caring for her.

She remembered how Rick hadn't liked the thought of his sister being with Liam, had worked to come between them.

"You didn't like me with Hope," Liam pushed, oblivious to the effect his words were having on Steffy. "It's like you can't stand for anyone else to be happy."

Happy? Steffy felt like laughing. Yet again, this was all about Liam and his happiness, his desires.

Her gaze settled on the elegant silver candelabra in the center of the booth. She wanted to pick it up and hit Liam over the head with it. How could he not see what he was doing? How could he not understand how his words would make her feel? Steffy's eyes flicked from the table to Rick's face. She expected it to mirror Liam's closed fury, but he was looking at her, his eyes locked onto hers, blue and sad and careful. He squeezed her arm again.

"This is not about you, Liam," Rick said, and Steffy could tell he was working hard to keep his voice even. It sounded strained and unnatural, so different than the warm, laughing tone she had been enjoying for the last couple of hours. "This is about Steffy. And—" Steffy saw Rick swallow quickly. "And Phoebe. It's their day." Rick's face changed. His blue eyes darkened and the red mark on his cheek stood out sharply in the dim light. "For once, it's not about Liam Spencer and all his women."

Liam stepped forward and grasped Rick's shirt with his left hand, drawing back his right arm like a crossbow string, tensed for flight. His scowl deepened, his mouth open in a snarl of fury, and his eyes shot fire at Rick. Then his right hand shot forward, the fingers curled into a fist. It was like every bar brawl in every bad movie Steffy had ever seen.

Rick was not expecting it. He barely had time to try to step back and raise his own arms before the blow landed. Steffy heard the sickening crunch of fist on flesh and bone as Rick went down, crashing against the booth behind them. A woman sitting a few tables away screamed as Rick's head crashed against the wood.

"Stay away from her, Forrester," Liam snarled.

But Rick was not down for the count. He lurched up, advancing on Liam. "Why, Liam? I thought that was your job. To stay away from her when she needs you."

Steffy tried to get her body between them again, but it had gone too far. Liam rocked back onto his heels as Rick pivoted forward, the left side of his face now sporting a bloody cut close to where Caroline had left her mark. He shoved Liam hard in the chest, knocking him off balance, before drawing back his own fist and smashing it into Liam's scowling face. Before Steffy could blink, Rick had landed another blow, this time with his left fist. Steffy was astonished at the power behind it. She had never known him so fit and muscular, and she could see that Liam was hurting as he fell back.

"Rick, no!" Steffy launched herself at Liam, lying on the floor, trying to cover him with her body. This was an uneven match. Liam was angry, and filled with righteous indignation, but Rick was a formidable opponent. And he was not a man who liked to be pushed.

Steffy dragged Liam up and stood between them. "Stop it," she begged again, seeing two more men advance on the little group from the corner of her eye. "This is ridiculous. I'm not some prize for you to be fighting over."

Rick held up his hands and his face cleared. "Hey," he said. "I'm not interested in fighting. But I'm not going to let him push me—or you—around."

As Rick said those words, Steffy knew he was right. There was something so determined and hard in his voice. She felt hot and sick at the violence that had erupted, but she also knew that Rick had been left with very little choice. He had been helping and defending Steffy, and then he had been left with no option but to defend himself. She didn't really understand it, and she loathed the violence, but a part of her also felt warm and safe, knowing that at least one person had her back today. And that person seemed to be someone entirely different from the Rick she had known before. Someone who was growing up, thinking about his actions and his responsibilities.

Her head swam as she tried to make sense of it all.

Liam's face was red and a bloody cut slashed the edge of one eye. He opened his mouth to retort as the maître d' interrupted. The man was dressed in an elegant back coat and he was a picture of restrained discretion.

"Is everything under control here?"

Steffy knew that anyone else would have been thrown out at this point, but she had seen the manager's eyes light up as they'd entered. Both Steffy and Rick were well known in Los Angeles, and he would have been thrilled at their patronage. The thought made her feel a little dizzy. The Forrester name again, opening doors and gaining advantages no one else would ever know. Even when they were having a fight in a bar.

"We're fine," Liam said tightly to the maître d'. "Just a little disagreement. Show's over."

"Thank you, sir," the manager said, appraising the bloodied faces of the two men. "Perhaps it's time to call it a night?" He raised an eyebrow and retreated.

Steffy stood uncertainly between the two men, trying to think through what she needed to do. Rick put a hand on her arm again, and the heat of his fingers burned through to her skin.

"I'll go and fix up the bill," he said and smiled wryly. "And clean up." He pointed at his bloody face. "Will you be okay here, Steffy?" He motioned in Liam's direction, not looking at him. "I'll give you some time, but I'll come back and get you, take you home."

Liam growled again. "That won't be necessary, Forrester," he snapped. "I can take Steffy home."

Steffy's skin prickled. "No, Liam," she said. How could he think she would do that? Leave Rick here, after all he had done for her today? After Liam had punched him for nothing more than supporting Steffy. The thought made a warm flush creep up her arms and neck. Liam was so used to Steffy wanting him, being there for him, he really thought he could do anything he liked, to anyone he liked, and she would still be his.

Well, things were different now. She was not some possession, least of all Liam's.

"I came here with Rick and I'll be leaving with him. Get the check, Rick, and I'll talk to Liam."

Rick gave her a last, searching look, as though checking she really would be okay if he left her, and then headed toward the bathroom. Steffy slid into one side of the booth, waving her hand at Liam to slide in the opposite side. Liam hesitated, then sat, reaching across the table for her hands. She handed him an elegant white linen napkin instead.

"Hold this to your eye."

Liam picked it up but didn't put it to his eye. The cut was bulging and angry, and the love and concern Steffy had always felt for him rose to the surface.

"I think we should get you some attention," she said. "That looks nasty and it's very close to your eye."

Liam shook his head, finally pressing the napkin to his eye to wipe the blood away. "It's nothing," he said. He carefully placed the cloth down, and Steffy was distracted by the dark red stain on the white linen. The sight of the blood made her tummy swim again. She had been on the edge of nausea all day, and now it threatened her again. So much to take in. This was such an important day for her; it was about Phoebe, and it was about her baby as well.

Steffy had come so far today. She felt like the pieces of her life were finally starting to make sense. Even though the split with Liam the night before had been awful, today truly had felt like a new day. A day she could decide to be different, to live differently. And Rick had helped her to see that. It was okay for Steffy to focus on herself, spend some time thinking about her loss, her baby. And Phoebe.

It had been a day where things had started to make sense. That despite all that happened to her, she was alive, she was here. The living had an obligation to the dead—to live fully, and well. It was time for Steffy's next chapter.

She had a plan. She was going back to Paris to finish this time of grieving and work on planning the next stage. She knew that she would have more freedom to do that in Paris than she would ever have in LA. In LA, she was a Forrester. In Paris, she was another foreigner, enjoying the beauty of the place. No one cared who she was. No one stared.

All these things had become clear to her today. Because of the trip to the cemetery. And because of Rick.

At least, they'd made sense until Liam arrived.

When she'd seen him standing by that booth, her heart had done its familiar flip. It was as though he owned a part of her; that he only had to say the word and she would be his again, whatever had happened between them. What was it about Liam that he had the ability to take all of her carefully constructed realities and turn them on their head?

He reached across the booth for her hands again, and this time she let him take them. His skin was warm and dry, and it was as though his hands were exactly the right size and shape for hers. These hands had held hers and placed a ring on her finger. Tears swam in her eyes as she remembered, and she swallowed hard and blinked, not wanting Liam to see them.

But as usual, he saw everything. She swore he could see right into her heart, it was so open to him.

"Steffy." Liam's voice cracked as he said her name and he picked her hands up and kissed first one then the other, very slowly and deliberately, holding her gaze as he did. "I'm sorry, I—" He shook his head, as though he were searching for the words. "Rick was right."

Steffy made a mental note to remember this moment, because she was almost certain they were words she would never hear again. She suppressed the urge to smile. It wasn't the right moment.

But Liam did smile. "I know it's not something I say often. But he was right about one thing: I haven't been there for you. And I'm sorry. It should have been me here with you today. I should have known. I should have offered." He paused, looking at his hands. "When I got your message, realized what was going on, put it all together, I felt terrible. I got here as quickly as I could. It wasn't hard to find this place, and I just wanted to see you, comfort you. Tell you I was sorry. For today, for last night. For Phoebe. And—" He drew in a shuddering breath. "And for the baby."

Steffy's heart almost stopped in her chest. A noisy rush filled her ears and she had to work hard to hear what he was saying.

"I should never have said the things I said last night, about the baby. About *our* baby."

Steffy nodded mutely. These were not the right words, not the ones she really wanted to hear. He had every right to tell her how he felt. But what she really wanted was for him to know her well enough to understand why she had done the things she had done. Yes, she had been foolish; yes, she had not thought enough about the consequences of her actions. But a man who really knew her would know that she would never deliberately hurt something, someone, she loved that much. He would know that she had been driven to those actions by the sight of the man she adored in the arms of another woman. And, most of all, he would be able to look at her and see how much she was hurting. How much she just needed to be held and loved. How great the loss was inside her.

It was as though Liam could hardly see her. Everyone else in her life looked at her and saw it all—the weight loss, the darkness under her eyes, the grief. Why couldn't Liam? Was he simply too close to her? Or was he too wound up in his own feelings, his own grief, his own ego?

After tonight, hearing him with Rick, hearing him talk about her as though she were some kind of trophy, and hearing his words about Hope, she really wondered. She had grown up watching her father love two women and watching the impact that contest had on those women, especially her mother. A teacher at her school in England had once told her that those who do not learn the lessons of history are doomed to repeat them. Sitting here, watching Liam trying to make up with her, she knew it was true.

Was she really content with that kind of life? Always wondering, in every moment, if Liam loved her, when he might grow tired of her, or when he might reconnect with Hope? Wondering if she was good enough, sweet enough—just enough?

But he did come for her. Just like she had always wanted him to. And now he was sitting here and apologizing. He was saying he understood. He had come to find her.

She looked into those hot brown eyes and remembered the rest of it. He had punched Rick, because he did not like his things being taken from him. Like a schoolboy.

Steffy tried to focus in on Liam's words as he started talking again.

"I don't know what happened today, between you and Rick," he said. "But I don't care. Whatever it is, I forgive you. I forgive you for all of it."

Steffy studied her fingers, wrapped in Liam's, and focussed on each breath. He forgave her. Surely this was what she had wanted. It wasn't just Liam who blamed her for the baby. She blamed herself too. Hated herself, in fact. But she knew now she had to get over that. She had known it standing at the cemetery, talking to Phoebe. And Rick had helped. Now she knew she didn't need Liam to forgive her—she had to work out how to forgive herself.

She needed more now. She needed him to understand his part in this. If they were ever going to have a partnership, he needed to understand that he had played a role too. That actions have consequences. That he had hurt her very badly, being with Hope.

She studied his face, impossibly handsome in the low light, even with the cut marring his boyish beauty. She was just not sure what she wanted right now. She knew one thing: she did not want to come to heel, to accept his forgiveness unquestioningly; to be the Steffy who had always been there, wanting him at all costs.

The he smiled at her and her breath caught in her throat. "But I won't share you, Steffy. I won't share you with Rick."

She startled at Liam's words. It wasn't like that. It hadn't been like that between her and Rick today. Couldn't he see that?

"Liam," she said, squeezing his hand. "You've got it wrong. Rick has been kind today, wonderful, in fact—"

He snatched his hands away at her words and refused to meet her eyes. "I don't care what he has or hasn't been, Steffy. I won't have him back in your life, *our lives*. You're going to have to choose. It's him or me."

Steffy's hands balled into fists. This was so unfair.

"I want you, Steffy. I want you back. I want to be the husband you've always wanted me to be. It's only you I want. I see that now. I saw that so clearly today, when I got your message, and then tonight when I walked in and saw you sitting here with him. I wanted to tear him from that seat and murder him."

Steffy blinked. Was that what this was all about—Liam Spencer, having to have it all, just like always? Liam needing to beat Rick? Liam needing to have exactly what he wanted, without anyone getting in his way?

She tried hard to focus on what Liam was saying, but the low rushing in her ears was getting louder.

Liam held her hands tightly, and looked into her eyes the way he hadn't looked at her for a long time—not since before the baby. "We can have whatever you want, Steffy," he said. "You know what we have together. I can make you so happy, baby. I know it. Anything you want. And if, in time, you want to have children. I mean—" He broke off, and Steffy's heart ached for him as she watched him try to find the right words, searching her face. "I mean, whatever you want. Children, or no children. But if you want them, we can work that out. This does not need to be the end of that dream for you, Steffy." He squeezed her hand hard. "There are other ways, you know that. And I just want to be here for you. To love you, whatever you want."

Steffy closed her eyes and let herself imagine it: a life with Liam and a family, in time. The security she had always craved. She had wanted time to work things out, to decide what it was she wanted. But she had always wanted Liam. Maybe he could help her work through it? Maybe he could be by her side as she learned to forgive herself, and start the next phase? Steffy felt hope spread like warmth and light across her skin.

"But I mean it, Steffy." Liam's voice was low and serious. "You need to choose. No more Rick. Not after today. I don't want you to see him again."

Of course. Liam would not share. Liam would not see that Rick had been a friend to her today. He was making demands on her that she had never made on him.

The warmth that had suffused Steffy turned to ice.

She shivered as she watched Liam's eyes on her face. "And what about Hope?" The words were out before she could stop them. She had always promised that she would not be that woman, the one her mother had been. The one obsessed with the other women. But here she was. "Will you stop seeing Hope? Will you never see her again?"

Liam frowned at her, shaking his head a little. "Steffy, this isn't about Hope. This is about—"

"Check's taken care of," Rick said, stopping at their booth. He looked down at Steffy with understanding eyes. "What would you like to do, Steffy? I can give you a lift, or you can go with

Liam, if you like. I totally understand." He was steadfastly avoiding meeting Liam's eyes.

"Yes, Steffy," Liam said, and Steffy heard it again, that challenge in his voice, the one that made her feel like the prize piece of meat he was fighting for. "What would you like to do?"

Steffy didn't doubt she loved Liam. Every cell sang when she was near him. But tonight, perhaps for the first time, she wondered if it was enough. Liam was asking her to decide, right now, if she wanted him. But more, he wanted her to reject Rick completely. Just because Liam could not bear to see them together. And yet Steffy had experienced so much heartache, watching Liam with Hope.

Her brain felt thick and fuzzy as she tried to work it through. She looked from one man to the other. It wasn't as though she was choosing between them, the way Liam positioned it. But she was being asked to sign up to him. Agree to his conditions.

Her heart wanted to say yes. *Yes, Liam. Anything for you.*

But her mouth would not form the words.

"I think I have my answer," Liam said, sliding from the booth and striding out of the bar without a backward look.

Chapter Six

Rick let Steffy sit in silence for most of the journey home. He concentrated on the road but kept glancing at her surreptitiously. She was quiet and still and obviously in turmoil. The shadows playing across her face made her look like a statue from the Louvre. She truly was breathtakingly beautiful, and something about how slender she had become, the sharp points of her cheekbones, and the dark circles under her eyes, gave her the air of a tragic heroine. He wanted to reach out and touch her. Take one of those long curls between his fingers and rub it, feel its silky sensuality. He could almost see himself running it across his cheek, pressing it to his mouth.

There was no getting away from it—there was no one on earth quite like Steffy Forrester.

Rick's head spun at the direction his thoughts were taking. How was this possible? He had long ago sworn off the Forrester women. He had done enough to them in the past, and there was no way Steffy or any of them could possibly take him seriously again. He felt another jolt at his train of thought.

He looked over at Steffy again, and the realization hit him. There were no halfways with this woman—she was the kind of woman who could become an obsession. For the first time, he understood Liam's madness when it came to her. Then he thought about how Liam had been similarly obsessed with Hope, and he felt his lip curl.

Steffy deserved better than that.

His sister deserved better than that.

But surely he wasn't thinking about himself? Today was not about him and Steffy, not in that way. It was about honoring Phoebe and perhaps, in the process, putting some of their own demons to rest. Something about Steffy at the florist this morning, so still and sad, had touched him. He wanted to make up for all the pain he had caused her and her family. But somewhere along the way, things had shifted. As he had watched her almost collapse in his office, struggle out of that sofa to confront Caroline, deal with her grief at the graveside, and then finally let go and start to relax at the little bistro, something had grown between them. Something that had perhaps never been there before. A new respect, and a new intimacy.

And when Steffy had let Liam leave without her, Rick had been even more surprised. He had been sure that Steffy would climb back into his arms the way she always did. The way Hope and Steffy *always* did.

And then there were the sketches. He had always known that Steffy was bright and talented, but seeing those sketches had taken everything he had understood about her to a whole new level. He felt as though he had a new insight into her beautiful brain, and he understood now. Finally.

There really was more to Steffy Forrester than met the eye.

But why did that make him want to touch her hair, and touch her cheek, and press her to him again in another of those bone-melting embraces they had shared at the bistro?

He couldn't hold it back any longer. He dropped his hand from the steering wheel to her knee. "You okay, honey?"

She didn't answer, but laid her hand over his own. He picked up her hand and held it, rubbing his thumb across the top of it. As he pulled up to the curb outside the smart apartment building, Rick squeezed Steffy lightly on the arm, startling her out of her reverie.

"Steffy," he whispered, feeling his throat tighten as she turned to face him and he was assaulted by the full ethereal impact of her beauty. Why had he ever let this woman go?

She too seemed to be in some kind of daze, and she shook her head as though to clear it.

"Steffy," he said again. "We're here, back at your apartment. Are you sure you're okay to be here alone?"

Steffy's eyes widened at his words, and a slow smile curved her lips as she raised an eyebrow at him. "Why, Rick? What are you suggesting?"

Rick felt himself flush, and was astonished at the boyishness of his reaction. "No, oh God, no, Steffy, I'm sorry, I didn't mean ..."

She punched him lightly on the arm as she leaned toward the door. "I'm only teasing, Rick."

Rick felt cool relief flood his system. Thank God. The last thing he needed today was for Steffy to feel like he was putting the hard moves on her. She didn't need that. She needed comfort. She needed to feel good about herself.

"I'm fine," she said softly, patting Rick's arm where she'd punched it playfully. A waft of that signature perfume of hers penetrated his senses and caught him off guard.

"Steffy, I—" The words were out before he even knew what he wanted, except that he didn't want her to go. Not just yet.

"Yes, Rick?" She smiled up at him so sweetly, that hot pink mouth almost the only thing he could see as he looked down at her. The urge to kiss her was almost unbearable.

What? What did he want to say?

Steffy, I don't want this day to end?
Steffy, you're beautiful?
Steffy, I'm sorry for all I did to you?

But he'd promised himself he wouldn't make this day about seeking his own absolution. He would ask Steffy to forgive him. And Taylor too, one day soon. But he wouldn't do it today. He didn't want her to think that he had some kind of alternative agenda.

He took a deep breath and smiled at her. "I'd like to see you in." He held his palms up. "No alternative agenda, I promise."

Steffy hesitated for a moment, then nodded and smiled again. "Thank you, Rick," she said.

He got out and walked around the car to the passenger-side door, opening it and offering her his hand so she could step out. He could feel how unsteady she still was on her feet as she gripped his arm carefully.

He guided her carefully over to the discreet lobby, where security and a doorman hovered expectantly. She paused by the revolving door and he turned to her, trying to formulate the right words with which to finish this remarkable day. But she surprised him, as she always did. She reached up and gently kissed his still-bloody cheek.

"I mean it, Rick," she said. "Thank you." The touch of her lips on the insulted skin was like a balm. He almost moaned as he felt them connect.

Rick saluted her and pulled her into a quick hug. He was about to move back to the car when he saw it: Brooke's car parked right in his line of vision. And Brooke stepping out, with a determined set to her mouth and a long black leather pouch under her arm.

"Rick!" His mother's voice was shot through with surprise and alarm. Rick felt himself pull away from Steffy as though he had been caught *in flagrante delicto.*

Steffy spun on her heel and took in the sight of Brooke advancing on her. Rick put steadying hands on her shoulders as he felt her sag against him.

*

Of all the people Steffy did not want to see today, Brooke would have to be close to the top of her list. Today had been hard enough, long enough, traumatic enough, without being faced with this.

She didn't mean to sag so pathetically against Rick when she saw his mother, but he had been hugging her seconds before. And he was there, real and solid, and the most convenient place to rest her tired body.

"Brooke." Steffy nodded and tried to inject warmth into her voice. Whenever Steffy saw that woman, she felt such warring emotions. While they'd become close when Steffy's mother was missing, Brooke was also enmeshed in all the most painful moments of Steffy's life. Then there was the lifelong rivalry between Brooke and her own mother, Taylor. Over her father.

Steffy knew Brooke was kind, and fiercely loyal. But she also knew that Brooke had broken Ridge's heart when he'd found those text messages to Deacon so soon after their marriage. Steffy had seen firsthand her father's sadness and loneliness in Paris.

Brooke always got what she wanted. And whatever she wanted today, she had come dressed for it: she looked a million dollars in a tight black pantsuit that showed off her formidable figure. The matching bejeweled Louboutins made her legs seem impossibly long, and her blond hair was swinging loose and girlish around her shoulders. She really did seem timeless, and Steffy wondered if she would ever age.

Brooke stopped in front of Steffy and Rick, and her soft gaze swept over them. "Hello, Steffy." She shifted the black pouch she had been balancing under her arm into her hands. "I've come to see Liam," she said. "A proposal we've been discussing. Brooke's Bedroom."

Steffy felt herself groan internally. Brooke was determined to be close to Liam, in business and in life. Steffy was sure she saw it as a way to further Hope's romantic ambitions.

"He's not here," Rick said quickly.

Steffy watched Brooke's eyes narrow, and felt Rick's hands grow firmer on her shoulders.

"And how would you know that, darling?"

"We saw him today," Rick said. "He's … elsewhere tonight."

"Oh," Brooke said, her voice gentle but her eyes wary. Then she paused. "My God, Rick, what's happened to your face?"

"Nothing," Rick said, as he stepped out from behind Steffy, his hand going to his face. "A little disagreement between Liam and me today."

Brooke seemed to suddenly still. Her eyes roamed over her son's face and then landed on Steffy's. "Rick, may I have a word with you?"

Rick stiffened and his jaw set. "Sorry, mother," he said. "I need to see Steffy to her apartment. She's had a hard day."

Brooke bit her lip and Steffy could sense her thinking about her next words.

But Rick was one step ahead of her. "You'll have to come back later, Mom," he said gently. "Or maybe make a time to discuss it at the office."

Her son's dismissal was the spark that lit the tinder. Brooke exhaled in a whoosh and stepped sharply closer to Steffy and Rick. "Honey," she said, brushing a speck from Rick's shoulder. She was so close Steffy could smell her perfume. "Are you sure you want to go down this road again? Don't you remember what a disaster this was for both of you last time?"

"Mother." Rick's voice was a raspy growl.

Brooke moved closer to Rick, reaching up to touch his face where the angry red cut glowed against his brown skin. "You've already been hurt. I don't want you to risk getting hurt again." She glanced back over her shoulder at Steffy. "Steffy will break your heart, even if she doesn't mean to. It's just how it is."

Steffy wanted to protest that she was standing right there, that she could hear everything Brooke was saying, and that she had no intention of doing anything to Rick. In fact, all she felt right now for him was gratitude and warmth. She wanted to let out the anger that bubbled within her, but overlaid across it was a deep, bone-numbing exhaustion. All she could manage was: "It's not like that, Brooke."

Brooke turned, her grip tight on the pouch she was holding. "Really, Steffy? How is it?" Her eyes flashed, and Steffy felt herself shiver a little at the worry and fear she saw in Brooke's face. "I've loved you, Steffy, and I've even defended you. But isn't it enough that you're ruining Liam's life? Do you need to ruin my son's as well?"

Steffy could not believe what she was hearing. She knew she had done some bad things in her time; hurt people, disappointed people. But was she really so awful that she deserved this? Steffy thought she and Brooke were closer than that. But as she watched Brooke light up with concern for her son, she saw what this really was. Mother love. Brooke was not trying to hurt Steffy. But for Brooke, blood would always be thicker than water.

It was just so unfair. Brooke herself had hurt Steffy's own father so deeply. She was a fine one to talk about wanting many men.

"That's enough," Rick said, stepping between his mother and Steffy. "Mom, I know you mean well, but you don't know what you're saying. You've no idea what's gone on today, and the last thing any of us need right now is a scene on the sidewalk."

But Brooke would not be silenced. She sidestepped Rick. "I do know what I'm talking about. I know some things about you, Steffy. I know you've had more than your share of sadness. And I'm so, so sorry." Brooke's voice broke as she said the words, and Steffy knew she meant them. "But I also know that Hope is much better for Liam than you'll ever be. Hope supports and nurtures him. She understands him. You just cause him heartache. You don't mean to, you're not trying to, it's just the way things are."

Steffy felt all her fury and desperation bubble to the surface at Brooke's words. She stared at her. "You know what, Brooke?" Steffy's voice was soft and deadly. "She wants him so bad? She can have him. You can all have him. You with your Brooke's Bedroom plan, and Hope with her support and nurturing. It's time to nurture me."

"Nurture?" Brooke's laugh was sad. "You tricked and trapped Liam with that baby, and then you couldn't even do what you needed to do to protect it. I really hoped that you might have changed, Steffy. For your sake. For your own happiness. But you're the same dangerous, wild, spoiled little girl you always were."

Steffy's heart hammered in her chest, and she felt fury—cold and brittle—lance through her. "Don't you dare bring my baby into this," she spat. She knew it; she knew what she was without Brooke telling her. But she couldn't bear to think about the baby.

Brooke ploughed on. Her eyes were shiny with fear and anger. "When you have a child yourself, Steffy, you'll understand why I want to protect mine." Brooke shook her head, then held Steffy's gaze. "I'm sorry, Steffy, but you're poison to whoever you get near."

Steffy's skin tingled and her mind whirled at Brooke's words. My God. This really was how people saw her. How Brooke saw her. Her vision began to blur, but she would not cry in front of Brooke. She needed to run, to get away. Before she did something she would really regret. Her hands balled into fists and she felt she might explode with all the pent-up sadness and fury coursing through her.

As Brooke took a step toward her, Steffy became aware of a small crowd gathered behind the glass doors of her apartment building.

"Stop it, Mom," Rick said, his voice very low and very angry.

But Brooke wasn't finished. "I'll never let you have my son."

Steffy's world tipped and tilted in the wake of Brooke's words. She needed to get away from her—now.

"Don't say another word, Mother," Rick said, putting his arms around her, trying to move her away from Steffy. He pointed at his mother's black car behind them. "Please go. Go and think about what you've said and done tonight, Mother. Sometime soon I'll tell you about what Liam did today, and you might think some more before you speak and act. Before you jump to his defense." He released his hold on her.

Brooke stood before her son, eyes wide and face flushed. She couldn't meet his eyes.

Steffy noticed another person was standing very close to Rick, a short, squat man she recognized too well. He was wearing lurid purple jeans and round, wire-rimmed glasses and carrying a huge camera that was flashing insanely at the scene before him. He was a member of the paparazzi, the one who most constantly dogged Steffy: Angelo Antigua. At one point, she had been afraid that he was obsessed with her. Wherever she went, whatever she did, he was there, snapping away. His pictures were frequently featured in the most trashy gossip magazines.

Steffy closed her eyes and remembered that this was personal for Angelo. Steffy's father, Ridge, had recently bought the paparazzo off when he had caught perhaps the biggest prize of them all—a picture of Steffy, tearstained and broken, leaving the hospital after she had lost her baby. Even though security and her assistant had all worked hard to keep her face out of view, Angelo had caught the money shot: Steffy, head bowed, about to step into the limousine, frozen in a moment of pure, cosmetic-free grief.

Ridge had fought hard to win the photos back, but Angelo had known their value. The part that had hurt the most was that Ridge had only managed to secure the deal by arranging a meeting between Angelo and Steffy for her to personally thank him for his understanding.

The man had a knack for capturing people at their lowest and most vulnerable points. Like now.

"Smile, Steffy," he wheezed, and Steffy saw it all as he would capture it. As it would appear in tomorrow's columns: Steffy, dazed and exhausted; Brooke, anxious and tearful; Rick, holding his mother in a gesture of protective concern that could easily be twisted into something uglier.

Before Steffy could think of the right words, Rick roared like a bull in Angelo's direction and the man took off, Rick hot on his heels. He had fifty pounds and twenty years on Rick, but he also had the rat cunning of the street on his side—and a healthy respect for life and limb. Steffy blinked as she watched Angelo skip up the alleyway nearby, dodging dumpsters and scattering crates behind him as Rick pursued him. Then they disappeared into the alley.

Steffy turned back to Brooke. Her face was ashen. She looked suddenly small and lost, standing on the street corner as a crowd of faces gaped at her from behind the lobby doors.

"Today is the anniversary of Phoebe—of Phoebe's ..." Steffy trailed off as she sought the right words.

"Oh." Brooke seemed to deflate as she registered Steffy's words. "So the two of you ... He went with you?"

Steffy nodded.

A tear rolled down Brooke's cheek as she looked at Steffy. "I just want him to be happy."

Steffy read Brooke's message loud and clear. She understood why Brooke would see her as a threat to her son's happiness. Perhaps an even greater threat than Steffy had been to the happiness of her daughter, Hope.

Steffy felt sick and raw inside as she stood on the sidewalk next to Brooke and thought about all the things she had said. That Steffy was spoiled and wild. That she had tricked and trapped Liam. That she knew nothing about nurturing. And then of course, that other thing. The thing that clanged over and over in Steffy's head like the chimes of doom: that she had been unable to protect her own baby. Those words from Brooke, that Steffy knew were unusual for her, came from a deep, angry well of mother love that Steffy would never know.

Finally, Rick returned, panting. He stopped by his car and locked a black bag in the trunk, before jogging back to the women. He looked at his mother warily. "It's sorted," he said.

Brooke exhaled noisily, and at last all the fight seemed to go out of her. "Will he...?"

"No." Rick shook his head decisively, and Steffy realized that she'd been holding her breath until that moment. "We had a conversation," Rick said, smiling darkly. "His camera met an untimely end."

Steffy's hands flew to her mouth. *Oh no.* Rick had no idea what Angelo could do.

"Don't worry," Rick said to her, patting her shoulder. "We've reached a suitable compensation arrangement."

Steffy's stomach lurched at the memories Rick's words brought up. She knew just how much Angelo's silence cost.

"Thank you, Rick," she said. Her head was swimming with all that happened. "I need to get inside." The exhaustion that had threatened to take her over had been replaced by something far darker, and she needed to be alone with it.

"I can take you in." Rick's blue eyes sought hers but she was far away from him right now.

"No," she said, unable to offer him any warmth as the darkness started to take her over. "I ... I'm tired. But thanks again." She looked at Brooke, who seemed to have shrunk to half her usual size. "For everything."

Rick nodded, and turned his back to his mother so he could speak privately to Steffy. "Any time you need me," he said. "I'm here."

She nodded, knowing she should feel tired but instead just feeling those words drilling her brain. *Spoiled*. *Wild*. Dangerous to anyone who gets close to her.

Rick studied her face carefully as he picked up her hand and kissed it gently. "It's not true, you know," he said. "She's just afraid."

But Steffy knew he was wrong. She had tried all day to convince herself that life could be different, that she could be different. That it was time to move forward and that she could let go of the past. That she could allow herself to grieve, and love, and start afresh.

And then Brooke's words had brought the nonsense of all of that home to her. Steffy didn't deserve a second chance—she had hurt too many people.

She pulled her hand from Rick's and turned and walked toward the lobby. Security had managed to clear away the spectators and she walked to the elevator unmolested. As she stood at the doors, the words swam around in her head again.

Wild. Spoiled. Dangerous. Only capable of offering hurt.

And the deepest cut of all. Reminding Steffy about her baby.

Her heart rose up, raw and bruised under the weight of the words. She stepped into the elevator, feeling as though the walls were pressing in on her. Her breathing became sharp and short, her chest squeezing painfully. She banged hard on the little buttons to the penthouse. This was what she was. Steffy Forrester, wild child.

She could try to outrun it, she could try to change. She could draw pretty pictures and beg her sister's forgiveness. But she would always be the girl who didn't deserve love. And who would never have a child to share it with.

As she stepped out of the elevator into the penthouse suite, she thought about Brooke's face. The face of a mother protecting both her daughter and her son. A feeling Steffy would never know.

The huge apartment felt tiny and stifling, full of memories of Liam, even after the short time they had shared here. Another person she had not been able to live up to. Another love she had lost.

The red light on the answering machine blinked accusingly at her. She stood staring at it for long seconds before she stabbed it with her finger.

"Steffy? Steffy. It's me, Liam. I got your message. Where are you? I'm worried about you. I need to talk—"

Steffy poked the delete button quickly. She could not hear this, not again, not now. Her skin prickled and her chest seemed to squeeze each breath painfully.

It was too much. Phoebe, Liam, Brooke. It felt like the world was against her and she needed to get away. Her bones ached with exhaustion but she could not stay in this place that smelled like grief.

She ran into her bedroom, and tore the sharp suit from her body, changing quickly into leather pants and knee-high boots. She pulled on a black turtleneck sweater and a short jacket and ran back to the elevator. She banged hard on the buttons, willing the thing to come quicker. She could not be out of here fast enough. She needed to put some distance between herself and this place, this day.

She stepped into the elevator and jabbed again at the buttons, this time to take her down to the basement. The contented hum of the elevator was like a jackhammer on the raw places in her brain as it slid downward.

When she got there she almost lost heart.

She had not been on a bike since the day of the accident.

This thing had been delivered by the insurance company, not long after. A perfect replacement. Never, ever used.

It stood before her, sleek and black like a weapon. She knew now just how dangerous it could be.

The only difference now was that she didn't care.

Today she had told Phoebe that she would live, and live well, for her. But right now all she wanted was to be away. To feel the wind in her hair and the miles between her and LA. She wanted to be all the things they all knew her to be: wild; reckless; selfish. What did it matter what she really was, when everyone had already made up their mind?

She could not live in the prison she had created for herself.

Liam wanting her, but all on his own terms.

Brooke believing Steffy was hell bent on destroying her son, a second time around.

And Rick? The thought almost made her stop.

What about Rick?

What had happened between them today? Had it really just been friendship, comfort?

She closed her eyes and thought about how he had smelled as she had pressed against him; the soft, clean, earthy fragrance of him. How good his skin had felt, how hard his body had been as he had tensed against her in the little bar at the hotel. He had been there with her today, battling his own demons. He was trying to change, to grow. And he had stood up for her, stood up to his mother for her.

Steffy stood in front of the long, black, beautiful thing. Then Pedro surprised her with a small cough. "You want these, Ms. Forrester?" His smiling brown eyes twinkled at her as he held out the keys to the motorbike. "I've been keeping her in perfect condition for you. She's all gassed up and ready to go."

"I ..." What did she want? Coming down here, she had been sure. She wanted to ride away, far away, feel the wind in her hair and get away from all the things that hunted and hurt her. But now?

"You want the helmet?" Pedro held the helmet up, as sleek and black and dangerous as the machine itself. Steffy reached out for it, and the moment she felt it under her fingers, she was lost. It was like a drug. It didn't matter how hard she tried, she couldn't change. She might as well give into it. She needed to go, to outrun the ugly things Brooke had said to her. To outrun the confusing day. The labels she could never live down.

She placed the helmet on her head, swung a leg over the machine and inserted the key. As the bike turned over, she heard Brooke's words again, reverberating through her brain.

Wild. Spoiled. Dangerous.

She grinned at the little man as she revved the engine. "Don't wait up, Pedro."

He saluted her as she spun the wheels and fired off up the ramp. "No sir, Ms. Forrester," he agreed.

Chapter Seven

Rick turned to face his mother.

How could she not have seen what Steffy was going through today? Steffy had barely been able to stand up, she'd been so exhausted.

And right now, he knew how she had felt. He ran his hands through his hair and across his brow. It had been a long day, filled with sad moments and difficult encounters. Caroline, Liam, and now Brooke. Images from the day swirled through his mind.

Rick just could not understand why his mother had been so hard on Steffy. "How could you?"

"No, Rick. How could *you*?"

Warmth rushed to Rick's cheeks. He was not proud of the way he had spoken to his mother, but he also knew that in that moment, he'd had little choice. She had been verging on hysterical and he had been truly unsure what she might say or do next. He knew he could not let her keep saying those things to Steffy. Not today, after all Steffy had been through.

He sighed. "This is not about you, Mom," he said. He felt all his love for his mother fill him as he looked at her, scared and sad. He wanted to make her understand. "That girl—"

"*Steffy*."

"Yes, Steffy," Rick said. "Steffy, Taylor's daughter. The woman you have known since she was a little girl. The woman I—"

"The woman you what?" Brooke had a hand on one hip and a look in her eyes that Rick knew too well. This was not a woman who was used to being told what to do. She was good and kind, but she was also tough as nails. She knew how to fight for what she wanted, and what she didn't want. And right now, she did not want Rick anywhere near Steffy. Rick felt a primal scream rise in his belly and he clenched his fists to stop it from escaping in frustration at his mother.

"The woman I care about, very much. The woman who has lost a baby, and who went to the cemetery today to visit her dead sister."

Brooke stepped forward, and he could almost see the switch in her eyes as she held out her hands to him. "Darling, I am sorry for you. For you both. I can tell it's been a hard day." She chewed carefully on her bottom lip. "But you need to understand. It starts like this. I know what a kind person you are, at heart. You're drawn in by Steffy's sadness today. It's like that bird, remember? What did you call it?"

Rick frowned, trying to follow her train of thought. Then the mist cleared. "Toto," he said quietly.

"Yes." Brooke clicked her fingers. "That little old sparrow you'd found out in the woods, with the broken wing. You tended it so carefully."

Rick felt the old memories and emotions in his chest. Brooke had given him a little dropper to feed it with, and he had been so careful, so sure he could save it. He could only have been seven or eight, but he'd been certain that with time and love he could fix the tiny thing.

"And then it died." Brooke's voice was sad. "Despite your best efforts. Some things are just wild creatures. And no matter what you try to do to help them, you just can't save them. They can only save themselves. And even then, only if they really want to." Brooke was rubbing her hands up and down Rick's arms, as though he really was seven again.

But he was a grown man now, and he knew Steffy. He *knew* her. "She's not wild, Mother," he said, taking her hands from his arms and holding them gently. "And you hurt her just now. Can't you see how you hurt her? We've all done bad things." He looked right into those green eyes.

"All of us. But if we were never allowed to change, how might we know what else we could be? Where could we get redemption?"

Brooke nodded her head briskly and stepped back. "Fine," she said. "If that's how you want it." She smiled but he could see the pain and fear in her eyes.

He nodded back at her. "It is, Mother."

She stepped in to kiss him on the cheek and he kissed hers in return. He wondered briefly at why Brooke's casual dismissal of Steffy had hit him so hard. He thought about what he had just said to his mother.

Redemption.

That was something he really understood. He too had done some crappy things. He too needed to be allowed to start over, without the world judging him. Was that what this was about? He shook his head at the image of the injured bird that his mother had planted.

His mind skipped to the memory of Steffy's sketches. He closed his eyes as he saw them again. Ethereal and perfect. No. Steffy was not an injured bird. She was not wild. She was just ... beautiful.

The thought ignited something in him, a desperate urge to follow her, make sure she was okay.

"Goodbye, Mother," he said, feeling suddenly desperate to check Steffy was all right. "Are you going to be okay to get home?"

Brooke nodded. "Of course, honey," she said, smiling at him one last time before walking back to her car.

As he turned back to the building to go and check on Steffy, his gaze caught on a black motorbike roaring out of the side of the luxury building. The driver was wearing a sleek black helmet and long dark hair flew out from under it as she sped up the street.

His mind took a moment to catch up.

Steffy.

*

It felt good to have a bike underneath her once again. The wild machine was like a drug, and she loved and loathed it in equal measure. She had sworn she would never get on a bike again. And now here she was—in her hour of need a bike was a friend.

As she cleared the busy streets and moved out onto the freeway she opened it up, feeling the powerful throttle beneath her and the warmth burn into her thighs as she set off into the late afternoon sun.

Riding had always been a dangerous thrill, and now that she knew just how dangerous, the thrill was even sweeter. Because this was all she deserved, she deserved to risk herself. She didn't deserve the safety and security of a home and babies. Brooke had been right. Steffy deserved to walk the edge, alone and afraid. And even as she pushed the lethal machine harder, she knew it really was true. She was afraid.

Very afraid.

Steffy felt her palms grow slick. She remembered her first motorcycle instructor telling her that the fear was a fine balance: you needed it to keep you safe, but it could turn on a dime and bite you. It could shake your faith in yourself, jolt you out of the autopilot where your muscles and brain knew what they needed to do. In short, you could lose your nerve. And that's when you made mistakes. Steffy was moving dangerously close to that zone now.

But still she pushed the bike harder.

The events of the last twenty-four hours swirled in her mind.

The fight with Liam, and ending their relationship. Liam's brown eyes seemed to float just ahead of her, familiar and accusing. She changed lanes rapidly as though that might run the images off. The sharp swerve almost caused her to lose her balance and the feeling sent a dizzying spike of oxygen to her brain.

But still, her mind was determined to take her back over it all.

The dreams. Oh God, the dreams. She squeezed the throttle some more, closing her eyes for a second as the dream from last night pressed in on her. Trying to save Phoebe, trying to get her, and then knowing she was dead. Waking in that instant of blind, panicked twin instinct. Knowing her sister was gone.

As her eyes flashed open she saw that she had accidentally veered into the next lane. A protesting honk from a car that had to swerve to avoid her ramped her fear and fatalism up another couple of notches.

There was something sweet in this, though. Every time she had a memory, the risk and the danger jolted her to someplace else, a place where she had to live in the moment just to survive what she was doing.

Then the sketches. Those otherworldly things that seemed to come to her from nowhere. She was sure it had been Phoebe, speaking to her through her little charcoals. And the message had been about life, hope. Potential.

Next, she saw the cemetery in her mind's eye. She was standing at Phoebe's grave. The way those flowers felt, pressed to her face. She promised Phoebe that she could live, for all the years her sister would not.

The thought arrested her, made her aware again of her speed and the fragility of her skin. She eased back on the throttle. Rick had helped her see that too. He had told her that she was worthy of grief. That it was okay to take some time to feel the pain of the loss of her baby. He had looked at her as he had never looked at her before.

As though she was worthwhile. Truly special.

And, maybe, as though she could even be good.

She saw the sign up ahead, the turnoff she wanted. She needed elevation. She needed to see the sea, and the mountains. She guided the bike toward the drive she knew so well.

As she did, the memories of Rick stayed with her. He had seemed to want to be with her. She felt the press of his body against hers. The way he had looked at her in the limousine. The laughs and conversation at the little bistro. What was it that had passed between them? Was it just the echo of what had been before? Was it some kind of recognition of a kindred soul? Was it just shared grief?

She thought about how it had felt to be held by him, the fire that had leaped to life in her skin.

No, definitely not just grief.

The way he had looked at her, sitting across that booth, like he had all the time in the world for her.

She remembered his words: *Take as long as you like, Steffy. I'm not going anywhere.*

The memory warmed her as the bike turned toward the mountain roads. She could call to mind exactly how his eyes had looked, so blue and sincere, sitting across from her in that little booth as though they were ordinary people who could sit and chat about ordinary things. Not Forresters, with all that demanded of them.

The thought of the charming French bistro lasted only seconds, before the next memory assaulted her.

Liam. Dark and furious, turning his fears and anger on Rick. The sickening crunch of the violence. And knowing, yet again, that she was causing it all. And then Rick hitting Liam with the powerful punch that knocked him to the floor.

It was the two of them being men, being boys, of course, but really it was Steffy.

Brooke was right about her. Steffy was poison to whoever loved her.

She squeezed hard on the throttle and felt the bike leap forward under her hands. The road was curved and heavily treed, and she knew it could get even sharper and steeper as it climbed. But the ascent was good. It meant she had to focus on the road. Except it was so hard to concentrate when the memory of Brooke's words kept picking at her brain.

Brooke, so perfect and together, in that black pantsuit.

Brooke, so horrified by the image of her son with Steffy. So horrified that she had railed at Steffy.

And the things she had said.

Steffy's eyes squeezed shut again. *Wild. Dangerous. Spoiled.*

Then they opened as she tilted the bike expertly around a bend, enjoying the wicked sway. The next corner was even sharper, and she tilted the other way, her knee almost grazing the road. The next stretch of road was calmer, stretching out for a few miles before another ascent. But she snaked across the road, daring oncoming traffic to come for her.

As she did, she had a sudden wild urge to feel the wind in her hair. Her scalp and face were hot, burning up the road and weighed down by the memories pressing in on her. Steffy knew it was foolish but she felt she could hardly breathe under the weight of the helmet. All the safety lessons branded on her brain were powerless against the force of her desire to feel the breeze blowing through her hair, blowing away all the angst of the day. It was dangerous, but what did it matter? That was who she was. If she couldn't save her baby, why did she deserve to be safe?

Her baby.

Oh no, not that one. Not that memory. Let the others come. But not that one. She wasn't going there, not anywhere near it.

And she knew just how to chase the thoughts away.

Slowly, she released one hand from the handlebar and sat up a little straighter in her saddle. She unclipped the buckle underneath her chin, and immediately felt cool air lap at her neck. With trembling fingers, she pulled the helmet from her head and held it aloft. The sea breeze lifted her loose curls, and her scalp and neck tingled under the delicious assault.

Steffy felt wanton and careless. Like this, she could almost believe it didn't matter. That none of it mattered. That she could go as fast as she liked, and what would it matter? Who would even care if she died? Really care. Her parents, of course, but she had caused them their fair share of heartache.

She flung the helmet to the roadside with a vicious bellow, enjoying the sight of it bouncing along the green verge. She brought her hand back to the handlebars and squeezed the throttle again. She felt her skin tingle and her eyes sting as she saw the next ascent. The big yellow sign urged caution but she flicked her middle finger at it as she sailed past, Brooke's words hot and lethal in her brain.

Brooke was right. Of course she was right. Who was Steffy to think she could change, think that she could be redeemed? She was no good for anyone. Not Rick, certainly. And Brooke could see that at a hundred paces.

*

Rick leaped toward his mother's black Jaguar, knowing his car had no chance of catching up to Steffy on that machine.

His heart pounded so loudly he was sure his mother must be able to hear it as she turned to look at his face. "Mother, go home in my car." Rick pointed.

Brooke looked like she had a whole lot to say about that, but something in his face must have silenced her, because she simply gave a small nod and touched his arm. "Be careful, darling," she said.

Rick jumped into the Jag, wondering if he could catch Steffy, if he would even know where to look. He had a hunch, the way she'd been driving, that she would want to go somewhere she could really open the machine up. He headed for the freeway, his mind stuck on the look on her face as his mother had screamed at her. Haunted. Hunted.

He felt goosebumps rise on his arms as he imagined what she might do in the state she must be in. After the day she'd had. So much sadness and so many confrontations. The thing with Caroline. The ultimatum from Liam. And then his own mother. If Steffy died today because of this, he was not sure he would survive the guilt of it.

As he reached the freeway, Rick pressed the accelerator to the floor, heedless of the speed signs that littered the on-ramp. They didn't matter. None of that mattered.

He had to talk to Steffy.

He had to make sure she was okay.

The Jag's soft leather brushed his arms and he worked the stick and the pedals expertly. Rick pushed the car to its impressive limit, his eyes raking across the lanes, trying to spot a wild-haired girl on a big black bike, but there was nothing. He darted in and out of the traffic, swapping lanes to improve his visibility. A huge truck almost wiped him out at one point when he thought he spotted her in a far lane, only to discover the long dark hair belonged to a very large Hispanic man who looked curiously at Rick as he sped up beside him.

Rick was about to give up, deciding she must have gone another way altogether, when he had a thought. He punched numbers on the cellphone resting in its cradle. He knew the number by heart.

"Evans."

"Mister Forrester." The voice sounded like iron and tobacco. Rick immediately felt his heart rate settle.

"I need you to find a vehicle for me."

"Yes, sir." The best thing about Evans was that he never asked any questions. Rick could have said, "I need you to get information about the illegal trade in elephant testicles," and Evans would have said, "Yes, sir." It was just what he did. He was a fixer. He was on hand whenever Rick needed him to solve problems. Rick never asked how Evans got his information, or how legal it was, but he knew he could count on him. And that was what he needed right now.

Rick quickly rattled off what he could remember of the bike before hanging up, Evans' last words ringing in his ears: "Five minutes, sir."

Rick continued to shift lanes and scan the freeway furiously, his hope dwindling. She had to be okay.

The desire to know where she was, to know how she was, stuck like a poker in his chest. He felt so responsible for how she was feeling and for what his mother had said to her. Steffy acted so together, but after today, Rick knew just how vulnerable she really was. He just wanted—what did he want? He wasn't sure, but he knew right now that he wanted her to be safe.

As he swerved and scanned, memories of that other car trip pressed in on him. Phoebe, so angry, screaming, wanting him to stop. But he just wanted to get there. Phoebe, lashing out at him, driving her foot onto the pedals. And Rick realizing that he should have pulled over, that the situation was too dangerous and he simply could not control it. But it was too late. Well, it would not be too late today. It *could not be* too late.

Where the hell was she?

The metallic chirrup of the phone startled him. He glanced at the clock. Five minutes exactly.

"Sir. A bike matching your description exited the freeway four minutes ago at off ramp 101B."

101B. Rick's mind scurried. "That's …?"

"You're less than a minute from it, sir. Get into the right-hand lane."

"How do you know—"

"It's my job to know. Sir."

Rick finally felt himself exhale. He was only five minutes behind her. "Right. And Evans?"

"Yes, sir?"

"Thank you."

"My pleasure, sir. Now hurry."

Rick pulled into the right-hand lane and accelerated.

*

Steffy's head would not be quiet. It was like the ride was releasing some kind of floodgate, and all the memories that she had been trying so hard to put to bed were flooding out.

And it was not just the memories from the day either.

As she went faster and faster, feeling reckless and wanting to punish herself for all her mistakes, that day came back to her again; the day Phoebe died. Her internal voice was whispering to her: *It should have been you, not Phoebe.*

And she knew it was true. Phoebe had been good and sweet. Innocent. It was Steffy who had done the wild things, made the mistakes. Who had Phoebe ever hurt?

Steffy smelled pine and the sea as she navigated one hairpin turn after another. The unseasonal Santa Anas were whipping through her hair, driving her to go faster and faster as her thoughts spiraled out of control.

She knew she was finally coming down on the losing side of that battle her instructor had told her about; the battle to stay in control of your nerve, and your bike. But she was so tired. She could barely muster the energy to care. Because she knew it was coming. The reflections of the day, and on Phoebe's death, were all leading up to the grand finale. She could feel it, the thing she had been trying to outrun for the last two months.

The memory of that day.

She felt her palms slide on the handlebars and her lips sting in the hot, dry wind as the memory inserted itself into her mind.

The hospital.

The doctor telling her that her baby was gone.

And telling her the rest of it. That it was all done for her, there would never be any children. Lying on her side in the white, white room, on the white, white sheets and wishing she could see the blood. Wishing there was a wound she could look at, to prove it was real. That she was real. The gnawing emptiness, grabbing at her stomach and her womb, aching and taunting. Spreading her hands across her belly and feeling the flat warmth of it. Imagining as hard as she could that the little life was still there. Crying herself to sleep, and then waking and realizing it was real, that it had not been a nightmare. Her baby was gone.

A brutal hairpin turn loomed ahead of her. She could see the point where the road jutted out like a sharp elbow before turning back on itself. Huge trees decorated the verge and a big yellow sign screamed warnings to drivers about the perils of the place.

Steffy shook her head in the warm breeze and squeezed the throttle again.

*

At last, he saw her up ahead of him. She was taking the corners wide and low, avoiding the path of least resistance and treating the road like a race track.

Rick swore under his breath as he realized she had discarded her helmet, but he was also momentarily mesmerized by the sight of her hair flying behind her. She looked like some kind of mad Venus.

As the road bent, he lost sight of her again, only to catch her as he accelerated along the next stretch. He watched as her knee tilted dangerously close to the asphalt on the next bend. His breath caught and he wanted to call out to her, tell her she didn't need to do this.

The symbolism of it all wasn't lost on him. The motorbike. He knew enough about grief to know that this was classic self-blame and self-punishment. He'd been there himself. Oh boy, had he been there.

He just needed to talk to her again. Look her in the eyes and tell her she was good, she was worthwhile. Wrap her in his arms and tell her that he would stand by her and protect her, and—

What?

What the hell was he thinking? Wrap his arms around her? She was still married to Liam, for God's sake. And he'd only spent a day with her.

He shook his head to clear the errant thought, but he couldn't excise the vision of Steffy, still and sad, beside him in his car. The perfect line of that perfect mouth. As hard as he tried to remind himself that he had no business thinking about her mouth, it kept swimming before his eyes. And her eyes, so sad and so blue.

Why? Why was he doing this?

As he pumped the accelerator hard, Rick felt the car creep up to her. If he could just get in front of her, he could slow her down. Hopefully get her to stop, call out to her. But as he watched, the sleek black motorbike took on the ugliest hairpin so far. Her brake lights didn't even engage. He saw the car coming before she did. His extra distance gave him perspective she didn't have, and he could see it, barreling down the other side of the bend.

There was nothing he could do.

As he watched, a second or two shattered into a thousand pieces and felt like hours. There was going to be a terrible accident.

He was going to lose her.

As the thought settled in his brain, another overtook it. There was something he could do. He beeped his horn furiously, long and low and loud. The oncoming car swerved to miss the bike as Steffy swung out wide. The car missed Steffy but as she overcorrected, she lost control of the bike and it slid out from underneath her and hurtled toward a large tree.

She slid along the edge of the asphalt and then the roadside on one thigh, dangerously fast, before landing in a patch of grass.

Rick was seconds away. He screeched the Jag to a halt and leaped from the car, his legs like jelly as he ran toward her. The air was filled with the smell of petrol and smoke. He could see Steffy lying immobile on the grass, a long bloody scratch on her face.

Rick knew he was fast. He had been working out a lot lately while he tried to get his demons under control. He knew he could do a mile in six minutes, but if felt like it took an hour to cover the hundred yards or so between his car and where Steffy had landed.

As he ran to her, two realizations occurred to him. The first was that he could not lose her. Not the way he had lost Phoebe. Too much about this scene was familiar. It was a twisted déjà vu, and he just knew he could not take it. Not again.

The second was that his feelings for Steffy ran deeper than he had thought. Something had happened today. He had come to see and desire her in a whole different way. He wanted to be close to her. And not just as a friend. He wanted to offer her comfort and protection. He wanted to show her that she was capable of more. That she was good, and that she deserved love. Despite what Liam, Caroline, his mother said. He wanted to help her expel her demons, and maybe even let her help him with his.

But she was lying on the grass. So still.

Rick slid in beside her, falling to his knees and throwing himself onto her chest. Through the background sounds of the other vehicle, he could hear the dull thud of her heart. But it sounded weak, and her breathing was labored.

Oh God. Oh no.

"Steffy." He shook her shoulders gently but she said nothing. Her face had blood down one side, but she still looked beautiful. Her perfect lips were parted, and her eyelids were closed, highlighting each sinfully long lash.

He wriggled around behind her, calling out to the approaching driver of the other car to call an ambulance. "Do you have any first aid training?" The man shrugged, his face a picture of horror as he pulled out his cell and retreated.

Rick strained to remember what to do. Keep her flat. Keep talking to her.

"Steffy," he said, gently brushing the hair from one cheek. "Steffy, are you okay?"

Suddenly, he felt sure, very sure, that he was going to lose her. Just when he had found her again.

"Steffy," he said. "Steffy, don't go. Stay with me, honey."

Her body felt warm next to his but he wrapped his fingers around one tiny wrist and her pulse felt weak. "Steffy," he tried again. "Please be okay. I need you."

Her eyes fluttered open.

Chapter Eight

Steffy opened her eyes to see the gathering dusk pressing in on her. A harsh throb drilled into her thigh and buttock and sparks of pain danced down her right side. She smelled pine and dust and the sea, and the air felt too warm for this time of year.

Where was she? What had happened? Her hand flew to her stomach.

The baby! Was it okay?

As her fingers spread protectively across her stomach, awareness closed in on her, narrowing her vision to a pinpoint before she closed her eyes against the gnarled fingers of pain that clawed at her.

No. Of course. There was no baby.

She was Steffy, and all alone.

A great black fog of sadness filled her nose and lungs, choking and burning. Her baby. Her baby was gone. Tears stung her eyes and she felt the howl even before it was out—low and wild, like a shewolf whose cub has been taken. She didn't know where she was, why she was here or who she was with, but she knew that something that had been buried deep and safe inside her had been released. A kind of wicked genie she had worked hard to keep a lid on.

And now the lid was gone, and the thick ooze of pain and guilt and self-recrimination was pouring out. Out of her eyes and her heart and her brain, and most of all, out of her mouth. The wail broke her in two even as it assuaged the hot burn of grief inside her.

Gone. Her baby was gone.

Finally, she cried, grabbing hold of the body underneath her, tears pouring from her eyes as wild cries spilled from her mouth.

Then all the memories slid back into her brain as one: Paris, coming home, Liam, the cemetery, Phoebe, Rick.

Rick?

Steffy became aware of strong, warm arms wrapped around her and a low voice murmuring to her. "It's okay, honey, you're okay, you're gonna be okay."

Rick?

Even wailing and crying, she was aware that he wasn't telling her to be quiet. Wasn't trying to stop her crying. He was just holding her, half propped up in his lap. One big hand was rubbing her hair and her cheek while his other arm wrapped around her protectively. It felt good.

She struggled to sit up, but the drilling pain slammed her back down. She brought a hand to her face and then pulled it back, seeing the sticky red blood on her fingers like they belonged to someone else. "Rick?"

He was there, patting her hair. "You're okay, honey. The paramedics will be here soon. I think you're okay, but you've got a nasty scratch on your face and you've hurt your thigh. I think you should lie still."

She sank back gratefully onto Rick's hard thighs as the wailing subsided into hiccupping sobs. "I'm here, baby," Rick said, continuing to rub her cheek and her hair. "And I'm not going anywhere."

She studied his face upside down as he smiled at her. It was warm and bright, his cheeks flushed and his smile wide. He looked ... elated. "I thought you were gone," he said. "But I think you're going to be okay. Some bad knocks and you're going to be sore, but your pulse is picking up and your breathing is coming back to normal. Thank God." Dark blue eyes drilled into hers. "Thank God, Steffy."

Now she remembered all of it. How she had flown from the penthouse. The motorbike. The death wish that had slid into her brain as she had burned up the miles, taking each corner faster and wider, daring death, knowing she deserved it. How she had flung the helmet from her head, the last desperate act of defiance.

She didn't deserve Rick's care, his attention, his gratitude that she was unharmed. She didn't deserve any of it. Any more than she deserved Liam. Or the baby she had failed to protect.

She rolled herself off Rick's thighs and sideways onto the warm grass, facing away from him. "Go away, Rick," she muttered, her hands once again moving to cradle her belly. She breathed in the warm sweet smell of the grass and wished the ground could open up and swallow her whole, like in a fairytale. This was too hard. She was too tired. She didn't want to deal with any of it.

But Rick did not seem keen to go anywhere. In seconds, he had moved himself around to where she lay. He unfolded his frame and lay down on the grass beside her. Her irrational brain thought about how lovely his crisp white shirt was, and how dirty it was going to get, lying on the grass. She thought she should mention it to him. But a sudden shiver rocked her, even in the warm night.

Rick looked into her eyes and rubbed her arm with one big, warm hand. "You're in shock, honey," he said. "You're not thinking straight. Can you remember what we did today? Where we went?"

"Yes," she whispered, closing her eyes because his dark blue gaze was like a truth beam in her face and she knew she could not take it. "Of course I can. That's why you need to go. I remember all of it, and your mother was right, Rick. You deserve better. Much better than me."

Her voice caught, but she wouldn't let him hear it. Let him think her the same selfish, ungrateful Steffy she had always been. Let him think anything if it meant he would leave. He was right. He had grown up. He had really worked on the things about himself that had been vain, and jealous. He had become a better person. And he deserved better.

But Steffy? She was just poison. Poison to all those who loved her. A screw up. Surely Rick, of all people, could see that.

She ploughed on, knowing she had to make him believe her. "Today was ... just a moment." She swallowed, knowing now, in her heart, that it wasn't true. But knowing she needed to say it, for him. To give him a chance of something better. Maybe he could patch things up with Caroline. "We were just overwhelmed by our—" She stopped, closing her eyes again as she searched for the right words. "By our shared grief."

He raised himself on one elbow, still stroking her arm as he shook his head vehemently.

Steffy opened her eyes. She had to convince him, and she couldn't do it lying there, refusing to look at him. She heard sirens in the distance and knew the interaction was almost over. They would be here in a moment, and tend her. She just needed to get this done.

"I get it, Rick," she said. "I know there was a ... spark." Oh, yes, she remembered that spark all right. That delicious leap of possibility that had sizzled between them. She crushed the memory mercilessly. "But it doesn't matter. It was nothing. An echo of a past love affair." She reached out to touch his face, her fingers creeping into his hair as though they had a will of their own.

Rick laughed. "Nice try, Steffy," he said. "I don't think so." He grasped the hand that had been in his hair and brought it to his mouth, turning it over and pressing a kiss onto the sensitive skin of her inner wrist. Even with a kettle drum playing a symphony at the back of her skull, her skin reacted, lighting up like Christmas at his touch. "Do you feel that?" he asked, the rough rasp of his beard scratching the sensitized skin of her wrist. "Is that a memory?"

No. Her heart boomed inside her ribs as he continued the gentle assault on her inner wrist.

Steffy snatched her hand away as she heard the ambulance pull over.

Rick began to sit up, lifting himself on one arm. "Don't kid yourself, Steffy," he said. "And don't patronize me. Nothing about today was past tense. It was all very much now. And you know what else?"

Steffy shook her head, not trusting her voice as the aftershocks caused by his lips still raced through her blood. She felt molten and confused.

"I know you," he said, his voice so low and deep she felt it right in the center of her. "I realize now that I have always known you. We're alike, you and I. And once I would have thought that was a very bad thing."

Steffy heard the paramedics emerging from the van and making their way toward them.

Rick went on. "But not any more. There is nothing bad about you, Steffy. You've done things you've regretted. You know what? Big deal—we all have. Time to get over it and give yourself permission to be. To live. Fully and freely and without apologies. It's not so crazy what you did tonight. You've been bottling it all up. Phoebe, for years. The loss of your baby, for months now. Grief makes us crazy, Steffy. This—" He swept his hands around the scene, the twisted motorbike, the torn up grass. "This is pretty normal. And you." He touched her nose lightly. "You're normal too. More than normal. I've seen those sketches, Steffy." He touched her face gently as he began to stand up. "They're beautiful. You." He brushed one finger over her lips, seemingly mesmerized by them. "You are beautiful. Inside and out. No matter what anyone says."

Steffy's breath hitched at his words and at the dark and sensual tone in them.

"So you think I've changed?" She wanted to squash his mistake. *I haven't changed. I'm dangerous. Don't trust me, Rick. Don't trust in me. Don't want me.*

Rick shook his head as the paramedics covered the last few yards between them. But he didn't seem to care that they could hear what he said as they kneeled beside her. "No," he said. "I don't think you've changed at all. I think you're a sweet, sweet girl. And you always have been. Despite what anyone says. Despite what *you* say."

And then the paramedics were tending her and Rick moved back behind them. But not far, she noticed.

The paramedics carefully assessed her for head injuries, and bathed the scratch on her face, clucking and marveling at the minimal damage given her lack of helmet. They examined the bruises on her thigh and buttock. Steffy felt shame burn from her scalp right down to her toes. She knew what they were thinking: spoiled little rich girl doing what she wanted, leaving everyone else to pick up the pieces.

But something about the presence of Rick, hovering just behind them as they helped her over to the van, tended her wounds and ran some more tests, comforted her. Even though the thought of her stupidity shamed her, she clung to his words. She was sweet. She was normal. She was okay.

The paramedics fought hard to take her to the hospital but she knew right now it was more than she could bear. She just wanted to go home to lick her wounds and process all that had happened. Rick was siding with the paramedics, but she was adamant.

Finally, Rick ran frustrated fingers through his hair and sighed. He turned to the paramedics. "What are the risks of her going home?"

The elder paramedic shook his head. "There's nothing wrong with her except superficially," he said. "She's going to have a really sore leg for a few days, but the painkillers we've given her should help with that. We'd just really like to keep an eye out for signs of shock and concussion. Vomiting. Drowsiness. Hallucinations."

Rick nodded. "What if she came home with me? I could keep an eye on her."

"No." Steffy put a hand on Rick's arm. "No, Rick. I'm fine. I'm going home."

The paramedic shook his head. "Uh uh. You leave solo, lady, and I'm going to have to ring it in."

Steffy turned to Rick, who shrugged meaningfully at her.

She nodded, and felt something tug deep and dangerous in her tummy at the sweetness in those blue eyes.

*

"They said to bathe the cut," Rick said, his mouth set in a determined line.

"I can get Mrs. Harrison to do that," Steffy whispered, looking mutinously at Rick as he held up the new dressing. The air between them was charged with electricity. She wasn't sure what would happen if she really did let him tend to her wounds.

"I gave her the night off," Rick said quietly.

Steffy narrowed her eyes at him. Maybe Rick hadn't changed that much—he always had an eye out for an opportunity.

He laughed at her. "Shame on you, Steffy. She has a sick child," he said drily. "What do you take me for?"

"I'm not sure," Steffy replied, wrapping the fluffy dressing gown Mrs. Harrison had given her more tightly around herself as she sat on the stool facing him. But she smiled as she said it because he looked so offended.

"C'mon, Steffy," Rick said, his eyes wide. "It's been a long day. You need to go to bed. And despite what you think, I'm not so hard up for a lover that I would jump on you in the state you're in."

Steffy worked hard to squash a little whine of disappointment that threatened to spill from her lips.

As though he could read her mind, Rick smiled. "You may not be so safe tomorrow, so keep that gown handy. It's so frumpy it's almost a chastity belt. Where did Mrs. Harrison find that thing?"

It was Steffy's turn to smile. "Hmm," she said. "Well, I'll try not to be offended that I look like a grandma."

Rick lowered the arm holding the dressing. "Oh no, Steffy," he said, very slowly and carefully. "I said the dressing gown was frumpy. You, on the other hand, could be wearing a terry-cloth robe and shower cap and still make the cover of *Sports Illustrated*." He swallowed, then smiled quickly, as though he needed to change the subject.

Steffy smiled back at him, and turned her face so he could access the scratch, closing her eyes. "Okay, Florence Nightingale," she said, trying to keep her tone light. "Bathe away."

Steffy heard Rick drag in a deep breath. He had already set up a bowl of warm water and disinfectant beside his makeshift dressing station, and she saw him dip a cloth into it before she felt the warm sting on her face. "Ouch."

He stopped. "Too sore?" His voice was a little ragged, but she could tell he was working hard to keep it light.

Actually, the feeling was exquisite, sore but soothing all at once. "No," she said. "No, it's nice, keep going."

He started again, building up a rhythmic pattern. Dip, press, stroke. She kept her eyes closed and made friends with the sting just to enjoy the silken drag of the warm material against her sensitized skin.

Dip, press, stroke.

"So." She cleared her throat. "I hope I'm not keeping you from anything important."

Dip, press, stroke.

Her skin warmed under his touch and the sting and ache abated a little. But her tummy didn't feel so comforted; it felt weak and watery as the stroking continued.

"For some reason," Rick mused, his voice seeming to become one with the rhythm of his hands, "nothing seems more important than this today."

Steffy thought about his words. "Because of Phoebe?"

For the first time, Rick stopped and a small whimper of protest escaped Steffy's lips.

"Sorry," Rick said, starting again.

Dip, press, stroke.

"Yes," he went on. "I think so. At least, I mean, I think that's how it started. When I saw you today, at that florist, it seemed that we were in exactly the same place, battling the same demons. And you seemed so ..."

"Messed up?" Steffy could only imagine how she must have looked, sitting there at the florist.

"Beautiful," Rick said, carefully applying the new dressing before smoothing her hair where he had pulled it away from her face. As he did, the

Ros Baxter

slight tug on her scalp lit up Steffy's circuitry, and the brush of his warm hand on her shoulder didn't help either.

Steffy tried to focus on his words. "Losing Phoebe the way I did, it had a huge impact on my life. It was the turning point, really. The beginning of knowing I needed to be different. But—"

He broke off and stepped away from her. He was rubbing his eyes and she was hit by the realization of how difficult the day had been for him too.

"But it took me a long time, years, before I worked out how to do that. If there was one thing Phoebe knew about, it was following your heart. Today I decided I can be exactly who I need to be. Who I *want* to be. And that's okay. Life is short, and precious. All we can do is live in the moment."

"It was the same for me," Steffy said quietly. "The same, but different. Losing her, it felt like I'd lost a piece of me. She had always been there. When she was gone, I spun out of control. The times I've wanted her—" Steffy dipped her head, not wanting Rick to see the tears that formed in her eyes. She did not want to cry, not again. She took a breath. "The times I've wanted her to be around. Just to see her, laugh with her, tell her something. Most people are born into this world alone, and we learn to let others in. It's not like that when you're a twin. Your first experiences, your earliest memories ... they're all of being part of something bigger than you."

Rick nodded, reaching out to touch Steffy's cheek.

"Why do you keep doing that?" she asked.

"Because it's so soft," he said. "And I can't help myself." He picked up one long curl and settled it back on her shoulder. "Go on," he said. "I'm listening."

Steffy chewed on her lip, trying to get the words exactly right. "Today, at the cemetery, I thought I'd found some closure. I talked to her. Does that sound crazy?"

Rick shook his head and stepped closer to her. "Nope," he said. "I still do it sometimes."

Steffy bowed her head again, in case she really did sound crazy. She didn't want to see it in his eyes. "I told her I'd decided to make a better go of things. That I was going to live, for her. For the life she couldn't have."

"So what went wrong?" The little frown between his eyes was so appealing she wanted to smooth it with her finger. "Why did you go from that, to jumping on that bike and taking that risk?"

"What went wrong?" Steffy laughed a little. "What didn't? Liam. Caroline. Your mom. But she didn't need to do much. Not really. It was mostly me. My fears took over. I just had to get away. It all crashed in on me. I felt like I was ..." She shrugged.

"Worthless?" Rick's prompt brought the tears to Steffy's eyes again.

"Yes," she said. "I didn't care today, Rick. I really didn't. I just rode and rode, faster and faster."

"I know," he said. "I could see you. So close, and yet not. It almost killed me. I needed to get to you. I needed to tell you to stop. And to put your damn helmet on."

"Why?" This was the thing Steffy couldn't quite understand. Why did it matter so much to him? Why did she matter so much to him? The thought occurred to her again. Phoebe. Maybe he really was just trying to make right the things he'd gotten wrong before.

He closed his eyes. "I couldn't let it happen again. I know how easily things can spiral out of control."

Steffy nodded. "I get it."

"No." Rick's eyes opened. "No, you don't get it, Steffy. It was also more, much more than that. What you and I have is different. I felt it today and I know you did too. I was a kid when Phoebe and I were together. We were kids. You and I are different now. We're all grown up."

As he said it, his voice lowered. Their eyes met and suddenly Rick was standing so close that she could feel his breath on her face, hot and sweet. Rick reached a hand to her face again, and then quickly drew it back. "Time for bed," he said, giving what looked like a forced smile. "You've had a big day."

Steffy knew it was true but it didn't stop the sinking drag in the bottom of her stomach as he moved across to turn out the lights.

*

Rick moved closer to her, his nakedness hot and hard against the soft satin of her nightgown. She could feel every hard muscle and sinew of him. His skin burned hers through the material. She ran her hands over his shoulders, lingering on the bone there, before trailing her fingers lightly down his arms. His biceps flexed under her touch.

His head swooped down and she waited for the kiss that she knew was coming. But his head dived lower, dipping onto one taut nipple and sucking it into his mouth. The sensation set off waves of shivers across her torso and down her arms—and lower.

Her hips bucked against the hardness below his hips and she felt herself grow wet as he pressed into her. She called out his name.

"Steffy."

The room swam and spun.

"Steffy, are you okay?"

Steffy sat up, disoriented and dizzy in the dark. Her leg ached and the unfamiliar room frightened her. It took a second or two before the pieces fell into place. Rick had taken her to his home.

And Rick was sitting on the bed beside her, not sucking her nipple.

"Steffy, you were calling out for me. Are you okay?" Rick switched on a low lamp by the bed. He was shirtless. The clock on the table read 02:19.

"Rick?" A freight train thundered through Steffy as she watched him, rumpled and sexy, his broad chest tanned and heavily muscled. He was right. They had been kids back then. And he was all man now. She shook her head to banish the thought. What was she doing, thinking about him like this? Last night she had been fighting with Liam. What had happened in a day? And what had that dream been about?

"I'm here, Steffy, shhh." Rick wriggled closer to her. He looked sleep-dazed as he held out his arms to her and she dived into them, clinging to his chest. "You just had a nightmare."

Steffy bit her lip against his warm chest. *Oh no, she hadn't.*

Rick hugged her hard, rubbing her back soothingly, like he would a child's. "You're safe here, just rest. You can stay as long as you like. As long as it takes you to sort out what you want."

Steffy felt a flare of guilt flash though her. She pulled away. "It's okay, Rick. I'm okay, honestly. I just always have strange dreams at this time of year."

He nodded. "I hear ya."

"Do you think you could just stay a while, lie beside me?" The words formed in her mouth before she could stop them. She knew she shouldn't ask, she knew it was a step too far. She also knew why she wanted him there. Her skin was tingling from the assault of Dream Rick and she wanted to be near him, no matter how dangerous it was.

Rick looked at her long and hard. He shook his head. "No, Steffy," he said. "I'm really sorry, but I just can't."

Shame coursed through Steffy. "Oh," she said. "Oh Rick, I'm so sorry. I didn't mean, I wasn't—"

"I know, honey," he said. "I know that. It's not you. You're perfectly entitled to need a little comfort right now. It's not you." He grinned. "That old line, huh? 'It's not you, it's me.'"

"Caroline?" Why did the vicious spike of jealousy rear its head as Steffy said her name? She had no right to it.

"What?" The word rose from Rick like a curse. "No, Steffy." He shook his head. "God, no. That's over. Long before today, if I'm honest with myself, but finally today, if you know what I mean."

She nodded ruefully, thinking about Liam's face as he'd delivered his ultimatum in the bar. She echoed Rick's line from a moment earlier. "I hear ya." Then she looked him directly in the eye. "So what is it?"

He moved closer, sitting so near to her that she could feel his hard thigh against hers through the starched white sheet. "Do you really, really not know?" His voice was a growl and he was a big cat, inching closer, trapping her with his gaze. "Do you really think I could lie beside you, like a nursemaid?"

She shook her head. "I don't know."

"Yes. You. Do." Each word was a hard nail of certainty. He reached up and grasped Steffy's chin, bringing her face close to his, slowly but firmly. "You know exactly what would happen if I stayed here with you."

Steffy swallowed, shivering as Rick's thumb stroked the side of her cheek.

"And that would be pretty great, actually," Rick continued. "Except for one thing. I don't want one hot night, Steffy. I don't know what I do want. But I know I don't want just one night from you."

Steffy nodded. She knew. She really did.

"Which means," Rick went on, "we need to talk. I need to really tell you what I've been feeling today, all day, more and more with each passing hour."

Steffy wanted to talk, wanted to tell him to keep going. He was so dear to her, sitting like that, shirtless and honest, offering her comfort even while he made it clear he wanted much, much more.

She wanted to tell him she had been moved by him too. That he had increasingly affected her as the day went on. That by the time he was bathing her wounds she was just about wild with caring and confusion and lust. But the words stuck in her throat.

"Steffy," Rick said, reaching out to touch her hair. He held a long curl in his fingers and stared down at it, rubbing its silkiness between his fingers like he was some kind of connoisseur, checking for quality. "You took a chance on me once before. And we had a beautiful thing. But it—"

"It was the wrong time," she said.

"Yes," he agreed, dropping the curl but picking up her hands and bringing them to his face, running her soft palms along the rough stubble on his cheeks. The sensation made her knees tremble.

"And now …" She looked at him, searching for the right words.

"And now it's exactly the right time," he said, bringing her hands to his mouth and slowly kissing each of them. "Could you ever—could we ever try again?"

Steffy remembered her promise at Phoebe's graveside, to make every moment count. She realized she saw Rick differently. Not as the cruel, jealous boy who had messed with her whole family, but as someone who really understood her. Someone she had history with. Someone who could love and protect her, who had been by her side all day.

"I think so." She nodded.

Rick moved his hands back to her face, grasping her chin again and pulling her toward him. His head dipped and his lips were on hers, firm and soft and warm and insistent. He parted her lips and the feeling of his tongue inside her mouth made her bones melt. She dissolved against him, running her hands across the hard wall of his chest.

Then she kissed him back. He was right. They weren't children any more. And everything she felt, everything she wanted to do to him, was all grown up. She pressed her lips into his, meeting his tongue with hers, using her teeth on that sensuous bottom lip of his, pulling and tasting and daring him to take it further. So much further.

He pressed against her and pushed her onto the bed. He stared down at her, his shoulders rising and falling with each heavy breath. His eyes swept across her and he shook his head. "You are unbelievably beautiful," he said. "Perfect. In every way. And I never want you to doubt that. Not ever again." He looked like a god, shirtless and flushed, his desire satisfyingly evident through his soft cotton boxer shorts.

She wanted to tear them off him, see him as she had seen him in the dream, naked and perfect. She wanted to touch him intimately, take him in her hand, hear him lose control. Over and over again.

"Steffy," he said, his voice hoarse. "I didn't mean—I don't think we should. It's been a long, hard day for you, and then the accident. You need to be sure you want this right now."

It was her turn to grasp his chin. She met his gaze steadily. "I've never been surer of anything," she said. She took his hand and used it to drag her silken nightgown up her thigh. Then she guided it gently to her panties, placing it on top of the soft material.

Rick groaned deeply. "Oh, Steffy," he said, slipping his fingers into her underwear. He kissed her feverishly, trailing his tongue and lips over her face, neck and chest, making his way relentlessly to the place he had been in her dream.

Maybe she really was developing psychic powers.

"Not here," Rick rasped.

Why not? It seemed like a good place to Steffy.

"I want you in my bed," Rick said, standing up and looking down at her with a stare so hot she felt the tiny hairs on her body scorch under his assault. "I want you in my bed. I want you in my life. I want you in my heart."

Tears leaped to her eyes at his words. He wanted her. All of her. He knew her better than anyone, and he still wanted her.

He held out his hand to her. "Do you want to come?"

"Yes," Steffy said, feeling the word echo in her heart and her head. And she realized she was right. She'd never felt surer of anything.

She stood and took his hand.

Rick picked her up as though she weighed nothing and held her close against his chest. Steffy's skin burned under his touch as he squeezed her hard against him.

"This is just the beginning, Steffy," Rick said, as he carried her to his room. "I promise."